BLIZZARD

A Sebastian Scott Novel

by Tee Emdee

Paradigm/SHIFT Books
Atlanta, GA

A Paradigm/SHIFT Original

First Paradigm/SHIFT edition, November 2014

ISBN-13 978-0692326602
ISBN-10 069232660X

Cover photograph: © Wikipedia

10 9 8 7 6 5 4 3 2 1

Manufactured in the United States of America

Table of Contents

For Corregan G. Brown
Above and beyond the call of duty.

ONE

Two a.m., Tuesday morning, in the China Basin. Very little moved at this time of night--or morning--in this part of San Francisco, not far from AT&T Field--home of the San Francisco Giants. One might see a rat, or a persistent patron of a nearby bar, but little else. Anchored boats rocked gently in the slight breeze as they nestled in their rented slips on this section of the Mission Bay marina. Carter Agee and Jordí Entrada conducted their long-arranged business meeting on one of these swaying boats. Both men stood in silence as one of Jordí's men walked around the cramped space below decks with a small box in his hand. The red lights on the display remained steady as the man swept the space and Carter's men--Carter included-- for recording wires, devices, or bugs. When he was done, he tucked the box into a pocket and replaced his hand on the submachine gun that hung from a strap on his shoulder.

"Do you have my money?" Jordí asked. A soft-spoken, burly man with short, curly dark hair, light olive skin, a narrow nose and lips, and cold, deep brown eyes, he could have been from Argentina, Abu Dhabi, or Arkansas. The lack of discernible accent in his speech gave no hint of his origins.

"You got my snow?" Carter met Jordí's stare with inscrutable brown eyes that glinted in the dim lights outside of the small cabin. He gripped the handle of an aluminum suitcase, while two others sat at his feet.

Jordí gave a short nod to one of the two machine-gunned henchmen standing behind him. The man stepped forward and used a knife to slit open one of the many boxes that helped crowd the small space. Bricks of an iridescent substance seemed to glow in the semi-darkness. Carter stepped forward and stuck his own pocket knife into one of the bricks. He held the small pile of powder on the tip of his knife to his tongue; it went numb and tingled only seconds after contact. While convinced that this was pure Blizzard, it never hurt to be sure--not with so much money on the line.

Carter removed a small black pouch from the pocket of his cargo-style blue jeans. He unzipped it to reveal three small test tubes and three bottles of reagents that were used to field test the authenticity of certain substances. He tapped a small amount of the Blizzard from the tip of his knife into each of the test tubes, then put a few drops of each reagent into each tube; one tube per reagent. When the tubes turned greenish-blue, dark greenish-yellow, and orange-yellow, respectively, Carter knew that the Blizzard was indeed the real deal, and that its unique mixture of cocaine, oxycodone, and methylphenidate were in proper proportions.

Carter nodded to one of the two men behind him, and that man lifted the two metal briefcases at Carter's feet atop the opened box. He flipped the briefcases open to reveal neatly banded stacks of non-sequentially numbered hundred-dollar bills.

Jordí grunted in approval and signaled to another henchman, who removed the stacks from the briefcases and loaded them into an automatic counting machine that had been undraped in the corner. Both Jordí and Carter's teams watched as the LCD numbers climbed upward with each machine reload. Finally, all three briefcases had been confirmed to contain the agreed-upon price of five million dollars, or $250,000 per kilo for twenty keys of Blizzard.

"Five million dollars seems to be a rather steep price, Mr. Agee," Jordí commented as his men repacked the money into dark duffel bags they'd brought along. "Being that we had to go through a lot of trouble to set up this meet."

Carter stroked his stubbly beard as he gave Jordí a thoughtful look. Carter's men packed the kilograms of Blizzard into the empty briefcases while Carter addressed Jordí's concern. "You've already received a discount of $10,000 per key, which is non-negotiable. I've already taken delivery of the product, so the deal is done."

"Do you know what I find interesting, Mr. Agee? I find it interesting that I have asked around my contacts in our particular field of expertise, and no one seems to have heard of you."

Carter shrugged. "I like to keep a low profile. It helps me live longer."

"Indeed." Jordí's dark eyes were impassive. "Yet your reputation precedes you as one who deals in quality product."

"My work speaks for itself."

"Mmm." Suddenly, Jordí chuckled. His men followed suit. "I agree with that sentiment. And I do not apologize for my suspicion; the federal law enforcement agencies in the United States have grown very savvy. One can't be too careful."

"True," Carter agreed. He hefted one of the briefcases. "Nice doing business with you."

"Likewise, Mr. Agee. I hope that we can cross paths down the road."

"You can count on it."

Jordí nodded and one of his henchmen moved to the door of the cabin. He listened before opening the door, then looked about the empty corridor for anything untoward. He gave the all-clear signal and waved Jordí and the other two men out onto the deck. Carter heard their footsteps as the climbed the stairs to the main deck above.

Jordí and his team moved quickly toward the wooden plank that led ashore, but not quickly enough. Night turned to day as bright halogen lights flooded the deck. Drug Enforcement Administration Special Agents stormed the boat, guns drawn and pointed at Jordí, Carter, and their respective people.

"DEA! Hands up! Drop the guns! Drop the bags! Drop 'em now! Show me your hands! Hands!"

Jordí slowly raised his hands in the air, and his three bodyguards followed suit. His implacable face belied his confusion, even as he was patted down and the semiautomatic gun in the small of his back was removed. How did the DEA know he was here? He continued to ponder this as he was handcuffed and led to an awaiting police car.

Carter was slammed face down against a barrel stenciled with the boat's name, *The Elegy*. A DEA Agent wrenched his hands behind his back and cuffed him. His Beretta .22 was removed from the waistband beneath his oversized shirt, as well as the backup gun in his ankle holster. Carter was frog-marched to a police car as well and shoved in the backseat. He watched agents and police officers carry contraband off the ship before he was transported to downtown San Francisco.

Back at the DEA headquarters, in the Little Saigon neighborhood, Jordí and his henchmen were processed and placed in separate interrogation rooms. Once they were safely behind locked doors and one-way glass, Carter's handcuffs were removed.

Carter rubbed his wrists to stimulate blood flow. "Is it me, or are handcuffs getting tighter these days?"

"It's you," one of the other Special Agents joked. Carter pushed the red cap off his head and scratched his close-cropped hair before flipping his middle finger at the joker, whose grin widened.

"No, it's Jomo," a third Special Agent commented with a smirk and head nod at the burly Special Agent who stood near the back of the room.

Jonah "Jomo" Modell shrugged, his muscles causing the straps of his bulletproof vest to creak. "Hey, I like a little verisimilitude on a bust with an undercover agent."

Carter paused in peeling off the fake beard and mustache. "'Verisimilitude'? Is that today's word?" Jomo's wife had given him a Word-A-Day calendar for Christmas.

"Don't knock a man for trying to improve himself."

The small group laughed as they watched Jordí sit alone in the interrogation room, staring at his reflection in the one-way glass with a preternatural calm. Carter continued to dismantle his disguise: he finally got all of the fake hair and adhesive from his face before removing the brown disposable contact lenses and tossing them in the garbage as well. He blinked his grey eyes rapidly as they adjusted to no longer being covered with thin discs of silicone hydrogel. Carter Agee was gone; in his place was DEA Special Agent Sebastian Scott. After being undercover for the past five months while he set up this buy, Sebastian was glad to be back in his own skin, so to speak.

He pulled off the oversized shirt to reveal a long-sleeved, navy blue thermal undershirt, which clung to his athletic frame. Sebastian left the room briefly for a much-needed bathroom break, then removed his personal cell phone from one of the many pockets in his oversized jeans. There were two text messages and three voicemail messages from Ivy Whitfield, his girlfriend. Sebastian sighed and started to check the voicemails, then decided against it. He already knew what the messages contained; no need to torture himself.

He and Ivy had initially met through a dating service over a year ago, but only started dating seriously not too long ago. All relationships have ups and downs but lately, they'd been in a down period--which Sebastian had a feeling was becoming more of a death spiral. He slipped the phone back into his pocket. He'd have to talk to her later.

Sebastian looked up as Special Agent Jason Kennedy, his partner of the past year or so, strode toward him with a brown paper tray of coffee cups from Starbucks. "Thought you could use one of these," Jason said as he removed one of the cups and offered it to Sebastian.

Sebastian gladly accepted the tall, white cup with the familiar green-and-white logo as he returned to the observation room with Jason in tow. "Thanks, Jason," he said before taking a deep gulp. Sebastian frowned at the cup; something didn't taste quite right. "Hey, Jason, I think you put a bad batch of milk into this. It tastes off."

"Oh, I asked them to put soy milk in it," Jason replied. His cheerful, ruddy face was as open and guileless as a child's. "Soy's better for you."

"Jason, if you ever mess up my coffee again, I will personally drop kick you into the San Francisco Bay. You know better."

"You'll thank me when you live to be ninety-five."

"I'm pretty sure I won't." Sebastian grabbed two slices of cold pizza from what was left in an open box on a nearby table, and washed down a bite with another sip of coffee, wincing at the plant-based aftertaste. He regarded Jordí through the one-way glass; it was now after five in the morning, he was in custody in a federal law enforcement facility, looking at long time based on the twenty kilograms of Blizzard--a designer drug made of cocaine, the narcotic oxycodone (better known as OxyContin), and the stimulant methylphenidate (better known as Ritalin)--he sold to "Carter Agee". Yet the man had yet to break a sweat.

He sat in the room as if he were expecting someone to join him for a meal, his fingers laced atop the table, his posture erect within the straight-backed chair. His attorney had arrived by this time, neatly dressed in an expensive bespoke suit and precisely knotted tie. The other man made urgent hand gestures while he whispered in Jordí's ear.

Special Agent Robert Grady, the Group Supervisor on the Blizzard task force, entered the room. The dim fluorescent overhead lights glinted on the scalp showing through his thinning hair. He introduced himself, then proceeded to question Jordí about his contacts, in an effort to get him to give up the name of his supplier. Finally, after over twelve hours of interrogation--and numerous interjections and objections by his legal counsel--Jordí reluctantly gave the name of someone higher up the food chain than he.

"That's my cue," Sebastian said as he rubbed his weary eyes. He looked forward to at least ten hours of uninterrupted sleep, a hot meal, and getting in touch with Ivy.

"Cue for what?" Jason inquired as Sebastian two-pointed his empty coffee cup into a nearby wastebasket.

"Cue for me to be outta here. I'm taking a few days' vacation time to attend a family reunion back home, remember? I'm leaving tomorrow."

"Oh, yeah. You want me to finish the paperwork on Entrada, then? You need to get some sleep, anyway."

"You don't have to ask me twice." Sebastian conferred briefly with Robert when he entered the observation room, clapped Jason on the shoulder, and left the building.

He squinted against the bright morning sun as he drove over to Guerrero Street in the Mission neighborhood where Ivy lived, and where he managed to find a parking space two blocks away. He could have called first, and probably should have, but he was afraid that the faults in their relationship foundation would widen beyond repair with yet another voicemail message or missed call. If he put off seeing her any longer, he might not see her for yet another few days. He walked to her building and looked up at the living room window of her second-floor apartment. Sebastian hoped she was awake; he'd lost track of her schedule as a paramedic, and he couldn't remember if she was on days or nights. If she was on days, then she'd already be up but if she was on nights, then she wasn't even home yet. He called upstairs and was glad to hear that her voice sounded awake. "Hey. You up?"

"Yeah," she said in surprise. "I'm on days. Where are you? You coming by?"

"I'm downstairs in front of your building, actually. I wasn't sure if you were home or at work."

"I'm just making some breakfast, so come on up."

Sebastian pressed the buzzer by her name and she buzzed him in immediately. He pulled open the wrought iron door and walked through the tiny foyer to the main wooden door, which had been propped open by one of the other tenants. Sebastian took the stairs to the second floor and knocked on Ivy's door.

"Hey," she greeted as she stepped aside to let him in. Sebastian caught the smell of bacon and his stomach rumbled. He noticed that while Ivy's voice seemed cheerful, her expression was neutral as she looked Sebastian up and down.

"Hey." He bent down to peck her lips, which yielded no discernible response. Sebastian straightened and looked down at the top of yellow satin scarf that covered her hair; Ivy was usually a very touchy-feely person, and he would have gotten at least a hug upon arrival. Something was definitely wrong. Ivy turned and went down the short hallway to her living room, leaving Sebastian to follow. She settled into a papasan chair, her purple sleep shorts riding up over her muscular thighs.

Sebastian took a seat on the neighboring sofa, which was upholstered in an interesting floral pattern. "I'm sorry I missed your calls and texts. This case has been pretty intense."

"I see." Ivy's brown eyes regarded Sebastian thoughtfully. "Sebastian, we need to talk."

"Okay," Sebastian said slowly. The phrase "We need to talk" never seemed to be a portent of good news. He tried to fight the fog of fatigue that wanted to wrap around him like a blanket, so that he could pay attention to whatever Ivy had to say. His stomach growled again, and he briefly wondered if it would be too rude to ask for some breakfast before she spoke her piece.

Ivy stared at the beige carpeted floor as she gathered her words. "How long have we been dating?"

"A few months."

"Five months, to be exact." Ivy continued to stare at the floor. "And during that time, while I have enjoyed your company, I would have enjoyed it more if I got to see you more."

Sebastian nodded to himself. He saw where this was going. He was only surprised that it hadn't happened sooner. "What do you want me to say, Ivy? I don't work a nine-to-five desk job; neither do you. You knew how my job was when we first started."

Ivy straightened and folded her arms across her purple T-shirt. "Even though I don't work a nine-to-five desk job, at least I know when my shifts will be over; and when they're over, they're usually over, give or take a few hours. I don't just not show up somewhere." Her eyebrows formed a vee of disapproval across the bridge of her nose.

"When have I not..." Sebastian cut himself off and pressed his lips together in frustration. True, there had been times when he had to break plans with Ivy, but he called to let her know. Usually. But sometimes, he couldn't. Criminals don't wait for you to make a phone call, or send a text, when they're about to be arrested. He sighed. "So what are you saying? What do you want to do?"

"I want to be with you, like we're a regular couple that spends regular time together."

"You want me to give up my job?"

"I didn't say that."

"That's the only way we can be a 'regular couple that spends regular time together.' I'd have to switch careers."

"Well, you can always transfer to another position. They have desk jobs in the DEA, right? You have an MBA; there has to be something else you can do."

Sebastian stared at Ivy as if she'd grown another head. "I don't want to do anything else, Ivy. And I can't believe that you're asking me to change."

"Didn't you get shot last year? And you almost died? That should have been a wake-up call for you, that maybe you need to pick a different career."

"Why? So I can take you out on Friday and Saturday nights?"

"Yes."

Sebastian rubbed a temple against the beginnings of a headache. "I can't promise you that. You know that."

Ivy nodded. Tears welled in her eyes, but her lips and jaw were firm with resolve. "Well, then, I think it's best that we go our separate ways."

Sebastian's expression was inscrutable. "If that's what you want." *So much for asking her to come to New York with me.*

"It's not what I want, but it's what I need." Sadness soaked her voice.

Sebastian's eyes turned the shade of a thundercloud. A comical phrase attributed to police officers popped into his head, even though there was nothing the least bit humorous about this situation: *Move along. Nothing more to see here.* He rose, and Ivy did the same. Sebastian reached out and ran a finger across one of Ivy's dark eyebrows, trailing it down her cheek to tap the faint indentation in her chin. "Take care of yourself, Ivy." He kissed her on the cheek and left her apartment, presumably for good.

As he drove the short ride home, he couldn't help but reflect on his sorry excuse for a love life. Most ended with complaints similar to Ivy's: he worked too much, too long, too sporadically for a "real" relationship. And, of course, being undercover a lot didn't help matters. He had no real, or rather socially acceptable, answer to a question as basic as, "How was your day?" Having to be someone else, so many times, had always been a bit scary. Not to mention, his profession included violence and death; he'd had to kill others in order to survive, and that's not something easily brought up, even in the dark. Sebastian lied for a living and the ease at which he was able to do so could be disconcerting at times.

The only person who never complained about his job was Nicole Bradford. He'd been involved with the feisty, shrewd Special Agent with the Bureau of Alcohol, Tobacco, Firearms, and Explosives, for over three years. She was the only one who understood the dark place that existed inside him, a place that came from seeing too much, doing too much, compromising too much. She never questioned that place; indeed, she had one of her own, which was part of why they were so good together--or so he'd thought. He quickly pushed thoughts of her out of his head. It had been two years since their relationship ended, and he had no idea why her hold on him remained. He didn't even know where she was; after their breakup, she'd transferred to the Baltimore field division of the ATF and dropped off the face of the earth. Although, he admitted to himself, it had been his choice to not keep in touch. He needed to go cold turkey from Nicole, or risk his sanity. She had gotten under his skin, and in his head, in a way that no woman ever had, and he doubted ever would. Nicole was like heroin, or cocaine, or any of the illegal substances he spent his career eradicating: highly addictive, bad for your health, but gave a high like nothing or no one else--a high that kept you coming back for more until you ended up broke and broken.

Sebastian trudged up the three stories to his apartment in a somber mood. As he crawled into bed, he hoped that his trip to New York would lighten things up. It would be good to see his family.

TWO

The majority of the floors dedicated to Quasar Financial Services was darkened and quiet, as one would expect at after ten p.m. on a weeknight. Only the light and movement from Nigel Pierre's cubicle dispelled the otherwise library-worthy conditions on his floor. He went back through the paperwork for the derivative loan swaps for both Cauldrice Properties and Landries Real Estate Group for the third time, and yet again he was confused.

According to their financial profiles, each company had a loan on their respective office buildings: Cauldrice had a fixed-rate loan, while Landries opted for an adjustable rate mortgage, or ARM. These two entities agreed to do a loan swap for five years. This was normal in the world of corporate real estate, and one of the many financial services that Quasar provided its clients. However, the normal interest rate on a loan swap of this nature was 5.75%, especially since the current London Interbank Offered Rate, or LIBOR, was .04214% for one year. Yet the interest rate listed on the paperwork for the Cauldrice-Landries swap was listed as 15%. Even though Nigel had little practical, real-world investment banking experience, having come to Quasar after a two-year stint at his family's food business, he still didn't understand why the interest rate was almost three times what it should be for a swap of this nature. He may not have been the brightest financial mind at the firm, but he knew when numbers were being padded.

Nigel shuffled the stack of papers until he found the signed contracts for services. From the very beginning, the inflated figures were pervasive throughout the paperwork, which meant that they were deliberate. Nigel even pulled up the electronic contracts to double-check, but they matched what was on the hard copies. That didn't bother Nigel; he had a younger cousin who was very good with computers, and he'd always told Nigel that a computer will tell you what you want, as long as you input the necessary data to produce your desired result; and that electronic files were rather easy to manipulate. But why? Who would put Quasar at risk with such a fraudulent transaction? If the Securities Exchange Commission found out, Quasar would be shut down, its Dun and Bradstreet and Moody's credit profiles would take a nosedive, and the Federal Bureau of Investigation would probably jump into the fray to investigate the possibility of fraudulent activity under the Racketeer Influenced and Corrupt Organizations (RICO) Act. The Internal Revenue Service would get what was left.

Nigel thought hard as he typed up his suspicions, copied and pasted supporting evidence, and saved it all to his personal folder on his hard drive. He made photocopies of the contracts and other paperwork and stuffed them into his satchel. He was ready to present what he had to someone who could actually do something about it, if his suspicions were true. But who? The lead on the Cauldrice account was Jeffrey Nixon, one of the junior partners at the firm--who happened to be the best friend and fraternity brother of Nathaniel "Trey" Jacobson III. Trey was the lead on the Landries account, the other junior partner, and the son of the firm's founder and Chief Executive Officer, Nathaniel "Nate" Jacobson, Jr. Nigel knew he had to tread lightly; accusing the son of the firm's owner and

21

CEO of wrongdoing would require airtight evidence. Right now, Nigel had just enough information to be dangerous, but nothing that couldn't be explained away, if you knew what you were doing. And Trey Jacobson had a very keen financial mind, even if he was a bit lazy. One false move could mean the unemployment line for Nigel.

Maybe Nigel should wait for Malcolm Jennings to return. Malcolm was a senior partner at Quasar and Nigel's assigned mentor at Quasar. He also had Nate Jacobson's ear. Word on the curb was that Malcolm was more of Nate's son, business-wise, than Trey would ever be; hence the friction between the two men. He nodded to himself; Malcolm would know what to do and since he and Trey were barely civil, Nigel wouldn't have to worry about Malcolm stabbing him in the back. Unfortunately for Nigel, Malcolm was out of town working on a loan swap between a museum and a shopping complex in Miami, Florida, and wouldn't be back in the office until the following week. He wouldn't take too kindly to Nigel contacting him in Florida, either; Malcolm's hair-trigger temper was legendary.

Nigel stretched and rose; he needed to use the bathroom before he got on the subway and headed home to the rented top floor of the Brooklyn brownstone where he and his family lived. As he headed down the hallway to the men's room, he heard voices coming from an adjacent hallway. Nigel frowned; the cleaning crew didn't arrive till around eleven o'clock, and they worked until three a.m. That particular long hallway housed the wing of offices for the Quasar executives, or E-Team, including Nate, Malcolm, Trey, Jeffrey, and Curtis Harris, the other senior partner. Nigel shrugged; it was none of his business. After relieving himself, Nigel was on his way back to his cubicle to gather his things when he heard the voices again, and the names "Landries" and "Cauldrice."

Curious, Nigel crept down the hall, past the empty desk of the executive assistant whom Trey and Jeffrey shared. His shoes were relatively silent on the thick carpeting of the executive wing. The conversation came from Trey's office, where light peeked through a crack in the door. Nigel got closer to listen.

"We good for tomorrow?" Trey's deep voice boomed. "Cauldrice is coming at 2, and Landries at 3:30."

"Why did you set the appointments for tomorrow?" Nigel recognized the quavery tenor as belonging to Jeffrey. "We won't have all of the money in time."

"Jesus." Trey's voice dripped with disapproval. "Jeff, you my boy, but I'mma need you to grow a pair."

"It's just...what if we get caught?"

"The point of using Quasar for this transaction is to avoid suspicion, correct? With a transaction of this nature, we never give all the money up front. We give them one payment tomorrow, and instructions on how to get the rest later. They'll give us our payment at the same time. Simple, fast, easy."

"What about Nigel Pierre?"

Nigel started at the mention of his name.

"Who?"

"The financial analyst on the account. Coming up on his second year at Quasar, used to work over in the Credit Risk Management department, under Nell George? Tallish, slim, quiet, grey eyes. Stares at Assata a lot."

"Oh, him." Trey dismissed Nigel in those two syllables. "Nervous Nigel. He jumps if anyone looks at him the wrong way. What about him?"

"He's the analyst on the account. If we leave him out of the loop, it'll look suspicious."

"I buried him in paper and sent him on a research goose chase. He won't bother us until the deals are done."

"What if he tells Malcolm? He's Malcolm's assigned mentee, after all."

"Tell Malcolm what? That a company executive gave him something to do while Malcolm is out of town? Nigel can whine about some kindergarten stuff like that if he wants to; he's only at Quasar because of the IPO."

"But if he figures out…"

"He won't. He can barely figure out how to do a PowerPoint presentation."

A jangling noise broke the ensuing silence. Nigel had heard that noise before; it happened when Jeffrey, who always kept his car keys in his pocket, jittered his leg in nervousness, which tended to be right before he had to give a presentation to Nate. "I don't know about all this, Trey…"

"What's there to know? You're the lead on Cauldrice, I'm the lead on Landries. It's quite normal, and even expected, for us to meet with our clients. As for the Blizzard, that's why we're doing things the way we're doing them, so there's no blowback on us."

Blizzard? Nigel's forehead creased in confusion. *It's October; we're not due to get any snow for a while yet.*

""I-I-I'm just saying that maybe we should do these deals another way," Jeffrey stuttered. "I mean, using firm funds is way too risky. I-I don't want to go to prison."

"Fine." Trey's voice was frosty. "You are more than welcome to keep slaving away for less than $200,000 per year, in a firm that will never reach the heights that any of the top-ten--hell, even the top-twenty-- firms will. So since you're having an attack of your conscience all of a sudden, why don't you just sit this one out? Meanwhile, you can return the over $5 million in inflated percentages that you've collected on previous deals. Better yet, why don't you call the IRS and tell them the number to your account in the Caymans, where those funds are hiding? I'll wait."

Silence, then Jeff said, "Trey, man...we're not just padding percentages to skim some extra off the top anymore. That, I didn't sweat because the way the U.S. legal system is set up, the most we'd get if we got caught is probation and a fine, maybe make restitution. But this...this is major, man. This is *Con Air* territory."

Nigel knew that *Con Air* was the name of a movie about hard-core federal prisoners on a hijacked plane; he'd seen it before on cable TV, and enjoyed it. A bead of sweat trickled down his spine. Were Trey and Jeffrey involved in something even more illegal than rigging a loan swap? Was it this blizzard? Was it occurring in a cold, snowy location? Quasar had clients in Sweden, Norway, Japan, and Germany; maybe whatever was going on had origins in one of those countries.

"Look, Jeff, haven't I looked out for you so far? This is what we were born to do, man," Trey cajoled. "This is what we deserve." His voice lowered with urgency. "I need you with me on this, man. I can't do it by myself, and there isn't anyone else I can trust with this."

Nigel heard Jeff give a heartfelt sigh. "Alright, man. I'm still in."

"That's what I like to hear."

The office door swung open suddenly, and Nigel stumbled backward up the hallway. The carpeting was so thick that Nigel hadn't even heard Trey approach his office door. Trey walked out and stopped short at seeing Nigel there. "Nigel," he greeted in a pleasant tone that belied the glower on his face.

"Uh, hi, Trey." Nigel tried not to swallow, but the nervous lump in his throat made him want to gasp for air.

"You're working late."

"Uh, yeah, just working on that research you gave me."

"You're a diligent man. What are you doing over here in the E-wing? Your cube is on the other hallway."

"I was using the restroom and I heard voices on my way back. I didn't know anyone else was here, this time of night, and I wanted to make sure that no one was trying to steal anything, or needed help in some way." Nigel knew he was babbling, but the look on Trey's face made him need to go to the restroom again.

"A company man through and through." Trey's gaze was cold and dark.

Nigel's stomach lurched. "I try to be."

The soft, overhead hall lights cast Trey's prominent eyebrow ridge in stark relief, making his eyes sink even farther in his face. The shadows lent an almost demonic quality to Trey's face. "You have a wife and kids, right?"

"Uh, yeah. Two kids, a boy and a girl."

"You should probably be at home with them. This is no place for a family man. I'm sure they'd miss you if something happened to you." Trey crossed his arms across his chiseled chest, and his biceps bulged beneath the sleeves of his pale blue dress shirt. He was a dedicated gym rat who still retained most of his football physique from his college days at Florida A&M University.

Nigel recognized that Trey was giving an order, not a suggestion, and the implied threat was equally clear. "I was just on my way out."

"Don't let me keep you."

"Right. Uh, good night." Nigel hurried back up the hallway toward his cubicle. He looked over his shoulder once and was disconcerted to see Trey still standing there, watching his departure. He logged off his computer, gathered his things, and left the building as quickly as possible.

Trey went back into his office, a thoughtful look on his face.

"Who were you talking to?" Jeffrey asked.

"Nigel Pierre. Speak of the devil."

"Nigel? What's he still doing here, this time of night?"

"Better yet, why was he outside my door, listening?"

Jeffrey frowned. "You think he was eavesdropping on our conversation?"

"Yeah. He tried to play it off like he heard a noise and was making sure everything was okay." Trey shook his head. "He's a poor liar."

Jeff's leg jittered again, and the jangling sound of his keys filled the air once more. "What are we going to do?"

Trey sat down at his computer and punched keys on his keyboard. "He said he was working on the research I gave him. Let's see if that's true."

Jeffrey came around the desk to look over Trey's shoulder. "You're hacking into his files? How? You don't have his password."

"I have everyone's password, except those on the E-team." Trey typed some more, then stared at his screen. "Hm. Looks like Nigel was working on a document that he saved about thirty minutes ago, on his personal folder on the company server." Trey copied the document to his hard drive, so that the time stamp wouldn't change on Nigel's end, and opened it. What he saw made his stomach clench. "Well, well. Nigel has been a busy bee."

Jeffrey's panic increased with each word he read over Trey's shoulder. "He was compiling evidence! I thought you said he wouldn't figure anything out?"

"He only has part of the picture. Still, if he's gotten this far, he could very well stumble across some things we've tried to keep hidden. I'm surprised he's gotten as much as he has. Maybe I've underestimated him." Trey leaned back his chair and stared at a replica of a 1970s lava lamp on the corner of this desk. Watching the green blobs slowly form and reform in the clear liquid calmed him down and helped him think. "We need to shut him down."

"How? He hasn't done anything that warrants disciplinary action, from a work performance perspective; besides, he'd fight it with Human Resources, which would bring more scrutiny upon us."

Trey stared at the lamp a while longer, then smiled a cruel smile. "I know what to do. Leave it to me."

~~~

Two days later, Nigel breathed easier as more time elapsed between his late-night encounter with Trey. Trey hadn't said anything to him since, other than to thank him for the assigned research that Nigel had completed and turned in. Nigel passed Jeffrey downstairs in the building lobby, but the other man didn't see him. Nigel was grateful for the lack of attention; being on Trey's bad side was not a good place to be. In fact, any negative attention from the executive team was to be avoided.

Nigel eyed the clock on his computer with relief, as the minutes wound down toward quitting time and the start of the weekend. He was especially looking forward to this weekend, as his grandparents were visiting from Trinidad for the first time in over ten years, and his family was having a reunion of sorts. Aunts, uncles, and cousins were traveling from all parts of the United States, and even overseas, for the occasion. This would be the first time that his grandparents would meet Nigel's children, their great-grandchildren, as well. As soon as Nigel finished the potential client profile he was working on, he'd go home, get his wife Priscilla and the kids, then head to his Aunt Janelle Pierre Scott's house in Brooklyn, where his grandparents were staying.

Nigel had just shut down his computer when he heard distant yells and gasps. Heavy steps thundered down the passageway outside his cubicle. Nigel looked up into the barrel of a handgun.

"DEA! Get your hands up! Up! Show me your hands!"

Nigel raised his hands slowly as he was yanked from his chair. His face pressed against the textured fabric wall of his cubicle as the DEA agent pinned him there; the gun was still pointed at Nigel's head. A second agent came in behind him and started rifling through Nigel's desk and his horizontal file cabinet, pulling out drawers and letting the contents spill across the floor.

"What's this about?" Nigel mumbled against the wall. "I didn't do anything."

"We got an anonymous tip that you were dealing drugs from your cubicle, Mr. Pierre."

"I beg your pardon?" It was hard to muster shocked outrage when your face was mashed against a wall, but Nigel managed to do so.

The second agent was now feeling around the empty spaces where the drawers once resided. When he got to the metal vertical file cabinet in the corner, he pulled at the middle drawer, which seemed stuck. "This seems to be caught on something." He managed to wedge his wrist into the narrow opening and felt around to find the source of the obstruction. He tugged until he felt something come loose, and the drawer popped open with ease. The Special Agent removed a brown paper-wrapped rectangular package, about the size of a fruit cake. He peeled back the paper to reveal iridescent whiteness. "Got it," he crowed as he resumed his search with renewed vigor.

His partner nodded and holstered his gun. "Nigel Pierre, you're under arrest for possession of cocaine with intent to distribute. You have the right to remain silent." The cool steel of handcuffs closed painfully around Nigel's wrists. "Anything you say can and will be held against you in a court of law." He frog-marched Nigel into the passageway. "You have the right to an attorney, and to have one present during any questioning. If you do not have an attorney, one will be appointed to you free of charge." By this time, they had arrived in the main lobby of Quasar. "Do you understand these rights as they have been recited to you?"

Quasar employees had poured out of their offices at the arrival of the DEA agents. Nigel's fellow cubicle denizens popped up and down, prairie-dog style, as they tried to peek over the cubicle walls to see what was happening. They whispered and stared at the spectacle of Nigel being hauled off in handcuffs. Other DEA agents darted in and out of Nigel's cubicle, leaving with his computer hard drive, boxes of documents, and books they'd taken from his file cabinets, drawers and tiny bookshelf. Yellow crime scene tape was draped across the opening to Nigel's cubicle after an agent left with one last box. Documentation declaring the cubicle as an official federal crime scene, under the authority of the Drug Enforcement Administration, and barring illegal entry, was affixed to the tape. Nigel searched the crowd for a friendly face but could find none. He noticed Trey standing in the rear of the crowd, his hands in his pockets and a self-satisfied smirk on his face.

"Do you understand these rights as they have been recited to you?" The DEA agent shook Nigel's arm as the phrase was repeated. Nigel nodded as he struggled not to cry. He was shuttled past the shocked, tear-streaked face of Assata, the firm's receptionist, and out of the office.

THREE

Sebastian parallel parked his rental car and walked the two blocks over to the brownstone in which he grew up, right off Nostrand Avenue in the working-class, predominantly West Indian neighborhood of Bedford-Stuyvesant in Brooklyn. A slight chill was in the October air, and he admired the red and gold leaves in the trees that lined the street. That's one of the things he missed in California: the obvious change of seasons.

He walked up the stairs on the leaf-free concrete stoop, noting the recent coat of red paint on the outer door; his father had obviously been busy getting the house in order for this reunion. Sebastian used his key to unlock the door and was met with the faint sounds of a steel pan over the slight throb of bass. He looked around the foyer, with its hardwood floors, and saw that his mother had redecorated again; more fresh paint, some new pictures on the walls, and a weird teal-and-purple glass figurine on the drop-leaf accent table along the center of one wall. He'd only taken a few steps toward the direction of the music when an attractive woman ran out and hugged him.

"Sebastian!" his sister cried as she placed a loud kiss on his cheek.

"What's up, Brat?" Sebastian replied with a grin. He picked his sister up and spun her around, before setting her back on her feet. "How'd you know I was here?"

"I saw you walking up the stoop from the living room window." Wistaria "Tia" Scott looped her arm through her older brother's as they slowly walked down the short hallway together. Brother and sister looked a lot alike, though Tia had brown eyes instead of grey ones.

"When you'd get in?" Sebastian asked as he sniffed the air. Someone was cooking, and his stomach reminded him that it had been a while since his two bags of complimentary peanuts on the last leg of his flight.

"This morning." Tia lived in Philadelphia.

"You drove?"

"Nah. Took the train. That way, I won't have to play chauffeur."

"That's cold," Sebastian chuckled.

Tia shrugged. "It's true. You know that most of the out-of-town relatives will want to go sightseeing, and I'm not trying to have all my time jammed up shuttling them to and fro. Anyway, I'm glad you're here."

"Aww, you missed me that much?" he teased. He placed a kiss atop her stylishly short, dark hair.

"Not really," she teased back. "But you haven't been home in over a year."

"True, but you just saw me a few months ago, when you were in San Francisco for that anthropology conference." Tia was an associate professor of anthropology at Temple University.

"For a few hours, and that's because you got called in to work."

"Oh, so I was supposed to tell the drug dealers that sorry, I couldn't make it to your drug buy because my sister was in town?"

"Yeah, you were. I am your favorite sister, lest you forget."

"You're my only sister, knucklehead." Sebastian tugged a lock of her hair, cut in a style reminiscent of the singer Toni Braxton on the cover of her first album.

Tia squealed and hit him in the side. "Ow! Quit it, Narc!"

"I got your Narc." He gave her hair one last tug for good measure. "Where's Mom?"

"In the kitchen with Aunt Michelle."

"And Dad?"

"I think he went to the store with Uncle Joseph. Mom's had him running errands all day."

They entered a room filled with people and music. A row of folding tables, covered with plastic red tablecloths atop which were stacks of white, red, and black paper napkins, plates, cups, and cutlery--the colors of the national flag of Trinidad and Tobago-- awaited the celebratory feast which was soon to come. Most of Sebastian's six aunts and uncles, along with seventeen first cousins, seemed to have arrived to welcome the elderly couple that sat in chairs near the empty fireplace. Sebastian dropped his carry-on bag in a corner and went over to greet his grandparents. "Hi Papa, hi Nana." He bent down to hug and kiss them both.

"Sebastian!" Benjamin "Papa" Pierre's voice still boomed, even though he was now a spry 83 years old. His wide, dark brown face was split with a grin, displaying slightly yellowed teeth that were still his own. "It's been too long. When are you going to give up this police business and come work for the family full time?"

"No time soon, Papa." Sebastian returned the grin, even as he knew that his grandfather wasn't joking. Sebastian used to work for his grandfather's business, Pierre International, in the summers during high school and college. All of the cousins did a stint in the family business at some point in time, although some still worked there in a full-time capacity.

Aarti Verhoeten "Nana" Pierre sucked her teeth and flipped the long, silver braid off her shoulder. "Mind yourself, Benjamin. Sebastian has better things to do than to run an old chutney company." She accepted the embrace of her grandson, to whom she'd passed down her grey eyes via her seven children. A gold stud earring winked in her small nose, which sat in the center of a barely wrinkled face that belied her eighty years of age. The combination of East Indian and Dutch genes had served her aging process well. "It's so good to see you, Sebastian." She held his face between her fine-boned hands, causing the myriad of gold bangle bracelets to chime softly around her slim wrist. "You look tired. Are you working too hard?"

"I always work hard, Nana," Sebastian replied with a wink.

"Have you recovered fully from your accident? I always told your mother that you went back to work too soon."

Leave it to his grandmother to describe his being shot and almost dying, over a year ago as just an "accident", like he'd dropped an egg on the floor. "I'm fine, Nana. And I got a clean bill of health before I was allowed back on the job."

Nana Pierre sniffed in disdain. "Hmph. Maybe you should come to work for your grandfather. It would be safer, and there are lots of pretty girls for you to meet in Trinidad. Good girls, from good families."

Sebastian leaned forward and kissed his grandmother on the forehead instead of replying. She'd definitely been talking to his mother; they'd been ramping up their matchmaking efforts quite a bit on his behalf, for the past year. His mother had been making a point lately of keeping him abreast of various engagements and childbirths within the family, not to mention every single female child of a colleague who was housebroken. "I'm going to let Mom know I'm here. I'll be back."

"You do that. We still have a lot to talk about."

Sebastian shook his head as he hugged and greeted relatives on his way back to the kitchen, many of whom he hadn't seen in years. He didn't see his favorite cousin, Jonathan Heath, or his best friend Alexander Townsend, so they must have not yet arrived. They were flying in from London, England and Los Angeles, California, respectively, so they might not arrive until later that evening, if not the next day. He was almost to the kitchen when a young man blocked his path.

"Hi, Sebastian," Michael "Trackie" Pierre greeted. His grey eyes shone with admiration for Sebastian.

"Hi, Trackie. How's NYU?" Trackie, so called because of his record-breaking achievements on his high school and college track teams, was a graduate student.

"I'm at John Jay now."

"Really?" Sebastian raised his eyebrows in surprise. He'd never pegged the twenty-three year-old Trackie as someone who would study at the renowned institution of criminal justice. "I thought you were studying to be a social worker?"

"I changed my mind. I'm getting my Master's in criminology."

"Okay." Sebastian didn't want to know what prompted the switch in his cousin's career plans. He probably watched too many cop shows on TV.

"You get any interesting cases lately?" Trackie had avidly followed Sebastian's career since Sebastian graduated with honors from the DEA Academy in Quantico, Virginia, over six years ago. He never saw Sebastian without badgering him for stories about his career.

"They're all interesting. Now excuse me, I have to go find Mom. I'll talk to you later." Sebastian beat a hasty retreat, or else Trackie would corner him and pepper him with questions for hours.

He entered the large kitchen, which his father had remodeled after Tia had left home for college. Janelle Pierre Scott had her back to the doorway as she stirred pots on the stove. Her identical twin sister, Michelle Pierre Warner, removed foil from large aluminum trays of oxtail, pelau, goat roti, curry chicken, shark and bake, and rice and peas.

Janelle turned at Sebastian's entrance. "Well, there you are!" She laid a spoon on the counter and went to give her firstborn a long hug.

"Hey, Mom." Sebastian pressed a kiss to his mother's cheek. When she finally let him go, he walked over to his aunt and repeated the gesture. "Hi, Aunt Michelle."

"Hi, Sebastian," she smiled at him. Her grey eyes, the same as her sister's and Sebastian's, glowed with pleasure. "It's good to see you. It's been a long time. You're looking well, but a bit tired."

"I'm still catching up on sleep. We did a bust a couple of days ago, and it took all night and into the next morning. Plus, I just finished a cross-country flight out here"

The sisters nodded their heads in identical gestures, and Sebastian bit back a smile. His family didn't quite understand what he did as a member of federal law enforcement, except that it had to do with drugs.

"Where's Dad?" Sebastian asked.

"He went with your uncle Joseph to get some more ice. Tia, get that sorrel out of the refrigerator and put it on the table. We're almost ready to eat."

39

"Yes, ma'am." Tia went to the refrigerator and removed large containers of a dark reddish-pink punch, made from the hibiscus flower. She made multiple trips in and out of the kitchen until they were all on the large table outside.

Stephen Scott and Joseph Pierre entered the kitchen a few minutes later, loaded down with bags of ice. "Well, look what the cat dragged in." Stephen's smile was as easy as his native Texas drawl. "Welcome home, son." He and Sebastian exchanged hugs.

"Hey, Dad," Sebastian replied with a grin. Father and son favored each other a lot, except for the eyes.

"Hi again, Daddy," Tia said on one of her repeat trips to the kitchen.

"Hey, Punkin." He gave his daughter a big kiss on the cheek before she toted yet more pitchers out of the kitchen.

"Sebastian, start taking these trays of food out into the living room, and put them on the side tables," Janelle ordered as she poured a pot full of callaloo into yet another foil tray.

"Yes, ma'am." Sebastian picked up the tray of oxtails and took it out of the kitchen. As he continued to ferry food between the kitchen and living room, the doorbell rang and he saw Tia go to answer it. She returned with a sour look on her face and a tall, well-dressed older woman in tow. A shorter, rounder, balding man, carrying two suitcases and two carry-on bags, brought up the rear.

"Hello, all," Victoria Pierre Heath stated aloud in a monotone as she swept a cool grey gaze over those assembled in the room.

"Hello, hello," her husband Reginald Heath sang in a British accent. He dropped the suitcases and removed a handkerchief from his pocket, which he used to mop his shiny, round face.

The cooling fall air clung to Victoria's brown wool shawl as she walked over and kissed her parents. "Hello Mum, Dad. I trust your trip was fine?" Victoria's accent was a combination of Trinidadian lilt and British crispness; she and Reginald lived in London, where he ran the London arm of the family business since retiring from a banking career at Barclays Bank.

"Hello, Victoria," Papa Pierre said as he kissed his youngest daughter. "The trip was fine. Your sisters have been taking good care of us since we arrived yesterday."

Victoria refrained from rolling her eyes as she kissed her mother on the cheek.

"How was your flight, Victoria?" Nana Pierre asked as she held her daughter's hand.

"Long, Mum. Joseph, Morris, hello," she nodded to her brothers, who sat near their parents. She ignored their wives.

"Hello, Victoria," Morris Pierre replied as he shook his head at his younger sister's dramatics. Some things never changed.

"Hey, Vicky, what's up," Joseph said cheerfully. He was only a year older than Victoria. He was also the only one who got away with calling her "Vicky", as she preferred to be called Victoria.

Victoria removed her shawl to reveal a sleek, hunter green sweater and skirt set. She searched the room. "Where's Brandon?" she asked, referring to the youngest of the seven Pierre children, and the sibling to whom she was closest.

"Brandon and Barbara called about an hour ago," Michelle said as she came from the kitchen, wiping her hands on a towel. "They've just left. They'll be here shortly, traffic permitting." Brandon Pierre, his wife and their youngest daughter lived in Philadelphia. His eldest son did as well, but Harrison Pierre was an emergency room physician and had long since left his parents' roof. She cocked her head and smiled slightly at her younger sister. "Hello, Victoria."

"Michelle." Victoria looked one of her eldest sisters up and down, noting the dark red velour tracksuit and unscuffed white canvas sneakers with red accents. She looked over at Janelle, who was also dressed casually in russet velour leggings and an oversized matching sweater, with black ballet slippers on her feet. "Janelle."

"Hello, Victoria," Janelle smiled as she went to hug her sister. She was the first of the siblings to do so.

Victoria returned the hug stiffly before noticing Sebastian. "Hello, Sebastian. You're looking well." Her cool gaze raked him up and down, and seemed to find him wanting. "You seem to have recovered nicely from your accident. Nice of you to grace us with your presence."

His mother's warning look caused Sebastian to swallow the snide comment on the tip of his tongue. Trust his aunt to consider almost bleeding to death a mere accident; she was like his Nana in that regard. "Hello, Aunt Victoria," he said with a half-smile. The only reason he tolerated her was because she was his blood aunt on his mother's side, and Jonathan's mother.

The sounds of objects banging into a wall and a woman's scolding voice floated in from the foyer. A man loaded down with luggage appeared in the doorway, followed by a younger woman. He placed the bags against a wall and entered the living room, rubbing sweat from his forehead. The movement caused the sleeve of his T-shirt to ride up on his right bicep, displaying colorful tattoos of the flags of Trinidad and Tobago and the United Kingdom, crossed at their staffs; and of various signs for the dollar, yen, pound, franc, lira, drachma, Deutschmark, and Euro. "Hello all," Jonathan Heath greeted the room, his British accent infused with cheer.

"Hi," Regina Heath, Jonathan's sister, added. Irritation was stamped across her brown face, which she removed when she went over to greet her grandparents.

Jonathan followed suit, then returned to the thick of the crowd. His gray eyes lit up at the sight of Sebastian. "Sebastian! Hello, old sod!" The cousins grinned and shared a hug and fraternal handshake. Jonathan, like Sebastian, Stephen, and most of the male Pierre cousins, were members of the same fraternity.

"What's up, Jon? Still multiplying Other People's Money?"

"I do what I can," he grinned. Jonathan was an international banker with Barclays International.

Sebastian looked over at Regina as she ambled over. "Hi, Gina."

"Sebastian." Regina's mannerisms and tone were eerily like her mother's.

"Hey, Jon! Hello, Gina," Tia said as she walked up with Carib beers for her brother and cousins.

"Hello." Regina looked her up and down with cool brown eyes. "I see you've finally done something with your hair. I suppose losing a few stone is next?"

Tia gave her a tight smile; she had indeed put on some weight after the breakup with her ex-man, Gerald, a few months ago. "And I see you're still a bitch."

"Sod off, Tia," Regina hissed. She tossed her long, blonde-streaked brown hair over a shoulder and glared at her older cousin before flouncing off.

"I apologize for Regina," Jonathan said. "She was dropped on her head as a small child."

"There's nothing wrong with that girl that a beatdown won't cure," Tia retorted. "You guys spoiled her rotten, and now we all have to deal with the consequences."

Before Sebastian could comment or take a sip of his beer, it was snatched from his hand. "Thanks much,

44

cuz, 'cause a brother was a bit parched." Dante Warner's grey eyes glinted with amusement as he tilted the bottle to his lips.

"Dante." Sebastian nodded coolly. The amusement in Dante's eyes faded at the subdued reception.

Tia still had no idea why things between Sebastian and Dante had been so frosty over the past few years, but she jumped in to keep the moment from turning awkward. "Hey, Dante!" Tia placed a loud kiss on his cheek. "Where did you come from?"

"I just got in." He took another gulp of beer.

"You flew in from Oakland?"

"Nope; New Orleans. I was at a biochemistry conference at Tulane." Dante held a PhD in biochemistry, and owned an environmental analysis firm in the Bay Area.

"Now, why didn't I get a kiss?" Jonathan demanded. "What am I, a second-class citizen?"

"Well, maybe if you were a citizen at all..." Dante began.

"Don't start, you tosser." Jonathan slapped the back of Dante's head.

"Okay, everyone, food's ready," Janelle announced. "Let's eat."

After Papa Pierre said grace, everyone dived into the food and the noise level dropped dramatically. Thirty minutes later, most of it was demolished as the family gathered around the foods they'd grown up eating.

Joseph Pierre kept checking his watch. "Priscilla, have you heard from Nigel?"

Priscilla Pierre, Nigel's wife, looked up from where she was wiping the food-smeared face of her two-year-old daughter, Maya. "I spoke with him earlier today, before he went to lunch." She wiped her own runny nose with the wipe before tossing it atop her empty paper plate.

"It's after six p.m. Shouldn't he be home by now?"

"He's probably caught in rush hour traffic, or his train is underground and he can't get a cell phone signal." Priscilla moved from Maya's face to her hands. "I know he said he was going to try and leave on time, so he could be here in time to see everyone."

Joseph grunted, but his forehead still puckered with worry. It wasn't like his son to miss a family gathering, especially with his grandparents in the United States for the first time in ten years. He'd always enjoyed spending time in Trinidad with them, and had been very excited that they were coming to the United States for a visit. He shrugged and went back to his food. Nigel was a grown man; he'd find his way to Brooklyn eventually.

At 8:30 p.m., Priscilla started to worry. Nigel had never been this late before, not without calling. She tried his cell phone again, but it went straight to voicemail. The four texts she'd sent him had also gone unanswered. Had there been an accident? She checked the websites of the *New York Post* and the *New York Daily News* on her phone, but there were no reports of any car or train accidents. The New York Metropolitan Transit Authority website also showed that all trains were running on time. Where could he be? She pulled a tissue from her pocket and wiped her nose again. A nauseated feeling flipped her stomach, and she pressed a shaky hand against it. She had a bad feeling about all of this.

Finally, she heard Nigel's ring tone, and his name and picture flashed across the screen of her phone. She answered quickly, pressing a finger against her opposite ear to block out some of the noise of people chattering. "Nigel? Where are you?"

"Pris?" Nigel's tear-streaked voice floated through the receiver.

"Nigel?"

"Pris..." Nigel began to sob.

"Nigel, what's wrong? Where are you? What's going on?"

"I'm in jail, Pris. I didn't do anything wrong, I swear."

"Jail?" The word came out in an incredulous whisper. Priscilla's legs weakened and she fell into a nearby chair. At the world "jail", the people nearest Priscilla turned toward her with interest. Someone hurried out of the room.

"The DEA arrested me, Pris. They said I was selling cocaine and using my job as a front. But it's not true! You know I don't do drugs, Pris, nor do I sell them. You have to believe me."

"I believe you," Pris whispered as her tears dripped down her face. Her nausea increased at the terror in Nigel's voice. She looked up at the concerned faces surrounding her and took a deep breath. "Okay, Nigel. We're going to get through this. Now, where are you and what do we need to do?"

"I'll need an attorney, of course, and bail money. I don't know how much yet, but it will be a lot."

Priscilla closed her eyes. While Nigel was making a decent income at Quasar, it was barely enough to keep them afloat. New York wasn't cheap, Priscilla didn't work outside of the home, and most of their savings had been put aside into college funds for Maya and her younger brother, Miles. Priscilla had received a meager inheritance from her deceased parents, but that had in the form of proceeds from the sale of the family home in her native Antigua and a few thousand dollars, which had been split among her and her three siblings. Suddenly, she felt justified in what she'd done. "We'll get it. Don't worry."

There was a murmuring on Nigel's end. "Pris, I gotta go. My time's up for the phone. But I'm here at the New York County Jail in Manhattan. My arraignment is tomorrow before the magistrate judge. So please, hurry."

Priscilla nodded on her end. "I will. We'll be there as soon as possible." She swallowed. "I love you, Nigel."

"I love you too, Pris."

~~~

Nigel hung up the phone before he started crying again. He stared at the dull reflection of his Day-Glo orange, jail-issue jumpsuit against the dirty white wall. As he was led back to his cell by the jail guard, he tried to figure out how he got pinned for this mess and how he could get out of it. Him? Trafficking cocaine? That was laughable. He didn't even touch so much as an aspirin, let alone illegal drugs. And he had no idea how that cocaine had gotten into his office. Nigel started to lie back on the thin, dingy mattress of the lower bunk bed, but decided against it; God knew who and what had been there before him. He opted to sit up and lean forward with his elbows on his knees, trying to think of something else he could do to save himself from this mess. He breathed through his mouth in order to keep from smelling the chemical odor of the open, stainless steel toilet in the corner of the 4' x 4' cell. At least he was by himself, for now, but this was Manhattan; the upper bunk could become occupied any minute.

Maybe his cousin, Sebastian Scott, could help. Nigel knew that he was supposed to be coming to New York to see their grandparents; he should have confirmed with Priscilla that Sebastian had actually arrived, since the nature of his job as a DEA field agent had led to Sebastian being a no-show at some family events in the past. Then again, Sebastian was also just as likely to let Nigel rot in jail. Sebastian had never liked Nigel, ever since they were children. He, Jonathan and Dante had been the big three, the Three Musketeers. Even though Jonathan was only two years older than Nigel, he fit in with the elder cousins in a way that Nigel had never been able to do.

He sighed. Thank God for Priscilla; at least she was in his corner. They'd met while students at Amherst College in Massachusetts and married shortly after graduation, while the then-22 year-old Nigel was doing a stint in the New York arm of the family business.

Maya had come along not quite a year later, then Miles a year after that. Even though Nigel was a married man, he still felt like he didn't get the respect the other men in the family did. His cousins, and even his parents, still treated him like he was a child. Working at Quasar had gained a bit more of their respect, but not much since he and Priscilla still occasionally borrowed money to help pay their bills.

"Lights out," a guard called. A few seconds later, there was total darkness, with only a smidgen of the dimmed fluorescent hallway lights seeping in through the bars. Nigel gingerly stretched out on the mattress and pulled the thin, dark cotton blanket over him. Tears leaked from the corner of his eyes as he chased sleep that never came.

FOUR

"I don't understand," Papa Pierre said. "Nigel does not have this in him. There must have been a mistake." Some nodded in agreement.

"Nigel is a good boy," Joseph said. His pipe smoldered in a nearby ashtray. "He's never touched drugs, not once in his life. And he's never stolen anything."

"He stole my Optimus Prime figurine when we were younger, but I won't mention that," Dante murmured in a voice that only those nearest him could here.

"Let it go, Tay," Tia advised as she tried to hold back a snicker.

"Well, they must have had sufficient evidence to arrest him," Victoria commented. "They didn't just pick him up on a whim. Don't these drug raids take time to coordinate?"

Sebastian kept his mouth shut. He knew all too well that the American jails were full of people who were incarcerated with no solid proof.

Footsteps echoed in the foyer, then a stocky man with close-cropped hair appeared. "What's up, good people?" Alexander Townsend said in his gravelly baritone. He clapped Jonathan and Dante on the shoulders and gave Tia a one-armed hug while kissing her cheek. He picked up on the somber vibe in the room. "What's going on? Something happen?"

"Alex!" Janelle walked over and hugged the man who was a second son to her and Stephen. Alex, a native of the Bronx, had frequently spent his Christmas and summer vacations with the Scotts during his college days, when he and Sebastian were roommates. "I am glad you're here."

"Glad to see you too, Mama Scott." Alex gently extricated himself from the death grip his surrogate mother had around his ribs. "Hey, Pops." He waved at Stephen, then looked back down at Janelle. "Now, what's going on?"

Janelle sighed. "Sebastian's cousin Nigel is in jail for possession of cocaine."

"Excuse me?" Alex blinked, as if he hadn't heard her correctly. "Nigel is in jail? For cocaine?" He'd had the misfortune to encounter Nigel on occasion, over the years, and he understood why Sebastian didn't like him. The man was whiny and weak, and loved to play the victim. Still, this was out of character for what Alex knew of Nigel.

"Yes. And he needs an attorney."

"Whoa, Mama Scott," Alex protested. He held up his hands in a "stop" gesture. "I practice family law, not criminal. Divorces, not drugs."

"But you passed the bar in New York, correct? And you've kept your license current?"

"Yeah," Alex said slowly. He had always figured he might end up back in New York someday, so he sat for the bar exam there as well as California. "But I don't have very much experience with criminal cases, especially of this magnitude." Alex hadn't so much as thought about a criminal case since he clerked for the United States Magistrate Judge at the Federal Circuit Court of Appeals in Washington, DC, after graduating from UC Berkeley law school. In Los Angeles, divorces were plentiful and allowed him to live the lifestyle to which he had happily become accustomed.

"You clerked for the federal court in Washington, did you not?"

"Yes, but that doesn't really matter for a local case. You just need a local criminal attorney who can handle this."

"Nigel got arrested by the DEA," Sebastian said.

"What?" Alex whipped around to stare at Sebastian. "Federal charges?"

"Yes," Janelle confirmed. "Can you sit in as Nigel's attorney until we find one that deals with this sort of thing?"

Alex cursed to himself. He really did not want to handle a criminal case, especially a federal criminal case, and particularly a federal criminal case with Nigel as a client. He also knew better than to cross Mama Scott, not that he wanted to. He loved her dearly; she was the mother he never had and he would gladly take a bullet for her. "I'll see what I can do," he hedged. He silently promised himself to call some folks he knew, and the American Bar Association, to find someone else who can take this case.

"Good," Janelle said as she stood with her hands on her hips. "Now that that's sorted, Alex, you can work with

Sebastian after he visits the DEA and finds out what happened."

Sebastian stared at his mother. "I beg your pardon?"

"You are going down to the DEA tomorrow and find out what is the meaning of these charges against Nigel." Her tone indicated that there was to be no further discussion in this matter.

Sebastian was expecting something like this. "First of all, Mom, I'm on vacation. Second of all, I work in San Francisco, not New York."

"But you're a federal law enforcement agent," Trackie piped up around a mouthful of roti. His metabolism was so fast that he ate around the clock. "It doesn't matter where you are based. You have jurisdiction anywhere in the United States and its territories."

"Did I ask you?" Sebastian glared at Trackie. Trackie smiled back and resumed eating. Sebastian looked back at his mother. "Thirdly, Mom, I can't just go over to the local field division office and ask about Nigel's case."

"Why not?"

"Because it isn't done, Mom. It'd be like sending a message that I don't think they know what they are doing, so I'm going to stick my nose in and help them do it. It's considered rude and poor form, professionally. From a law enforcement perspective, for all intents and purposes, it's none of my business. Especially since Nigel is a relative."

"That doesn't make sense," Lisa Pierre, Nigel's mother, argued. "What about professional courtesy?"

"Aunt Lisa, how does the DEA know that I won't tell Nigel, or anyone else, about his case? About evidence, strategy, or whatever I could to help him beat these charges?"

"Because you won't. You're just trying to help Nigel."

Sebastian shook his head in frustration. His family did not understand the way that federal law enforcement worked. "I can't do it," he said. "I'm sorry."

Lisa slumped with dejection in her chair, while Joseph put an arm around her to comfort her. Conversations buzzed around the room in low tones.

Alex walked over to Sebastian and they exchanged a complicated handshake. "Good to see you, man," Sebastian said. "As you can see, I could use some backup."

"Man, what did I just walk into?" Alex whistled beneath his breath. "I'm still tripping that Nigel caught a federal charge. How much did they find on him?"

"I don't know, but Priscilla said they got him on distribution and trafficking."

"Trafficking too? That's crazy. Nigel couldn't distribute a newspaper, let alone coke."

"Well, the feds think he could, and did, which is why he's sitting in the county jail right now. He's got a magistrate hearing in the morning."

Priscilla overheard Sebastian's latter comment, since it came during a lull in the room's conversations. "In the morning?" she shrieked. "Nigel said that he was being arraigned tomorrow! I thought it would be later in the day."

Sebastian shook his head. "This is a federal case, which means a preliminary hearing in the Magistrate Court. The magistrate judge tends to hold bail hearings in the morning. Court starts at nine a.m." He shot a pointed look at Alex.

Alex pinched the bridge of his nose. "Looks like I'll be making phone calls sooner than I expected." He pulled out his cell phone and started scrolling through his contacts.

Sebastian exhaled loudly at the evaporation of what he thought would be a pleasant, family-oriented vacation. The family orientation would still be there, but not quite in the way he'd anticipated. He *really* didn't like Nigel.

~~~

Alex sat in a room reserved for attorneys to confer with their clients. Because of the severity of the crime, he was allowed to visit with Nigel at this late hour of the night. He reviewed the DEA arrest report for the third time; he still couldn't believe it. Eight kilograms of a special form of cocaine called Blizzard was found in Nigel's office. Blizzard was a highly addictive mixture of cocaine, oxycodone, and methylphenidate-- better known as Ritalin-- and sold on the street for $2,000 an ounce after it had been cut with cornstarch, talcum powder, or any of the other household items commonly employed to stretch out pure product. The resulting high was so powerful, an ounce would last a mid-range habitual user for a month. Those eight keys of pure, uncut Blizzard found in Nigel's cubicle had a street value of over $5 million dollars. Alex groaned inwardly; Nigel couldn't have picked a worse time to get involved in drug trafficking, what with federal judges coming down harder on even first-time offenders. And, if he was not mistaken, it was an election year in New York. Unless he, or the new attorney, figured out something quickly, Nigel was looking at a the rest of his life in a maximum-security federal prison.

The door opened and the guard motioned for Nigel to walk into the room, then closed the door and stood guard outside it. The fluorescent lighting played over Nigel's wearied face. Alex was shocked; he remembered Nigel as a young, slim, decent-looking guy, with the Pierre gray eyes and a shy smile. This guy, however, looked as if he was ready to jump off the Williamsburg Bridge. A nervous tic had settled in and Nigel's left eye twitched at odd intervals, even as surprise flashed across his features. "Alex? What are you doing here?"

"Sit down, Nigel," Alex said gently. Nigel complied and stared at Alex out of eyes that seemed too big for his face. "I'm your legal counsel of record, to get you through the arraignment. We need to talk about what happened."

"You're my attorney?" Nigel asked in a dull voice.

"Just through tomorrow's hearing," Alex hastily amended.

"I thought you did divorces."

"I do," Alex said, "but your Aunt Janelle asked me to at least get you through the hearing on such short notice, since I have federal court experience."

Nigel nodded. "Then what?"

"Then we get you an attorney with more federal criminal experience." At the word "criminal", Nigel winced. "I mean, criminal court," Alex explained. "Not that you're a criminal."

"Then you're gonna get me out of here?"

"We're working on that, Nigel. Your family is getting your bail money ready. We'll find out exactly how much that is, tomorrow morning."

"Can Sebastian help?"

"There's not much he can do, if anything; the local DEA office here won't tell him anything about your case because he's a relative, and he works in a different office on the west coast. Plus, I can't tell him anything about your case without your permission."

"Well, you have my permission to talk to him. He may be able to help somehow."

"Okay. I'll let him know. But he still can't influence whether or not you get bail."

"I have to get out of here, Alex. I have to!" Nigel's voice cracked with unshed tears even as drops trailed down his cheeks. He leaned forward and grabbed Alex's lapels; the handcuffs glinted in the harsh lighting. "Do you understand me? I can't stay here!" He shook Alex to emphasize the point.

The guard looked through the door and saw Nigel grab Alex. He opened the door with his hand on the butt of his gun. "Hey! Sit down, Pierre!"

"It's fine, sir," Alex said as Nigel sank back down in the chair. "He's fine. He hasn't hurt me." Alex smoothed down his lapels in an attempt to defuse the situation and kept a wary eye on the guard. Nigel could not handle being put in solitary confinement.
The guard glared at Alex, then back at Nigel, before backing out of the room. He closed the door again but immediately looked through the large pane window in the door.

"I can't stay here, Alex! I just can't!" To Alex's horror, Nigel dropped his face into his hands and began to sob. "I can't, I can't, I can't," Nigel repeated through his fingers.

There were two things in his life with which Alex did not deal well: crying and monogamy. He removed a handkerchief from his suit pocket and handed it to Nigel. Nigel wiped his face before blowing his nose with loud honks. He held the balled-up handkerchief in his hands as he stared at the table.

"We're gonna get you out of here, Nigel, don't worry." Alex's voice was soothing; he could not handle Nigel flipping out on him again. "But first things first: you have an arraignment hearing tomorrow morning before the magistrate judge. We need to discuss your plea."

Nigel looked up at Alex. "Plea?"

"Guilty or not guilty."

The red-rimmed gray eyes hardened. "Not guilty, Alex. How can you even ask me that? Do I look like I would sell cocaine?"

"You'd be surprised," Alex retorted. "And this isn't about your innocence or guilt. It's about what the prosecution, which is the United States Government, can prove. And right now, they have a whole hell of a lot of proof against you."

"I didn't do it. I don't know how that cocaine got in my office. I don't do drugs, or sell them."

Alex sighed. "Alright. What kind of collateral do you have for bail?"

Nigel shrugged. "I don't know."

"Do you own your own home? Got stocks, bonds, Treasury bills? Got a car? A trust fund?"

Nigel shook his head. "We rent the top floor of a brownstone in Brooklyn. I have some stocks and bonds, but nothing major. I have no T-Bills, and I don't need a car. I live in New York." He scratched a stubbled cheek. "As for a trust fund, I don't come into it until I turn thirty-three. That's seven years from now."

Alex nodded slowly. He couldn't wait to pass this off to another attorney. Nigel was proving to be a recalcitrant witness--as well as broke--which was not helpful to his case. "Okay." He exhaled. "Do you have any relatives that live out of the country, or any real estate holdings in other countries?"

"I just told you that I don't own a home here, so what makes you think I own one somewhere else?"

Alex bit back a retort. He was beginning to remember why Sebastian didn't care for Nigel. "What about relatives that live out of the country?"

"My grandparents on my father's side live in Trinidad, as you know, along with my cousin Franklin Pierre. But they're all coming here. I have cousins in Toronto, also on my father's side, but we aren't close. They're outside children." The last was said with a hint of disdain.

"Outside children?" Alex frowned.

"They were born out of wedlock to a woman who was not my Uncle Morris's wife."

"Ah." Alex wasn't in the mood to explore the branches of the Pierre family tree. "Anyone else?"

"Aunt Victoria, Uncle Reginald and my cousins Jonathan, Regina and Christopher live in England. But they are all coming here except for Christopher, I think. He's an archaeologist, and he's on a dig somewhere." Now it was Nigel's turn to frown. "Why do you need to know all of this? What difference does it make where my family members live?"

"The court will determine whether or not you are a flight risk, which will influence whether or not you get bail."

Nigel's already ashen complexion turned grayer. "You're saying that even if my family gets the bail money together, I still might not get out of here?"

Alex sighed and prayed that Nigel would hold it together. "If the court determines that you have other places that would grant you asylum, be it a family member or a country's government, then the court is within its rights to deem you a flight risk and won't let you out of jail, for fear that you will run away. There are countries that do not have an extradition treaty with the United States."

Nigel looked as if he wanted to pass out. Alex quickly added, "I can make a case for you not being a flight risk. The judge may take your passport though, just in case."

"He can have my passport! I just wanna go home."

Alex shook his head again as he picked up the arrest report one more time and prepared to create a timeline with Nigel. The old saying was true: no good deed goes unpunished.

~ ~ ~

Sebastian lay in bed in his childhood room, but couldn't sleep; he was waiting for Alex to get back and fill him in on what happened with Nigel. He rose and went downstairs to the kitchen; he figured he could have a beer while he waited. As he arrived at the bottom of the stairs, the front door opened and Alex walked in. He looked weary, though his suit and tie were as impeccable as they were when he put them on a few hours ago.

"Was it that bad?" Sebastian asked.

"Bruh." Alex shook his head. "I need a beverage." He turned toward the kitchen and Sebastian followed.

Apparently, Dante and Jonathan couldn't sleep, either. They sat at the kitchen table with open bottles of Carib beer and Guinness stout in front of them, and plates of half-eaten leftovers. They broke off their conversation when Alex and Sebastian walked in.

"You look like Big Bubba strip-searched you, man," Dante observed.

Alex reached into the refrigerator and grabbed two cold Caribs, and handed one to Sebastian. "I can't wait to hand this off to someone else. Nigel almost made me commit homicide, right there in the jail." He took a gulp of his beer and sighed in satisfaction.

"Welcome to our world," Dante said wryly as he raised his stout in a salute.

"So what happened?" Jonathan asked.

"I can't tell you much, due to client privilege. But it basically boils down to he swears he didn't do it, doesn't know how or why he got arrested, and proclaims his innocence." Alex stared at his beer. "But I will tell you this: I hope you guys have a nice chunk of change handy, because his bail--if he gets it--will be steep. Without going into too much detail, he's in deep shit--deeper than you know."

"If he gets bail?" Dante repeated.

"If the judge deems him a flight risk--which is possible, given his family ties in Trinidad, Canada, and the UK-- Nigel could stay in jail until the trial. But he doesn't have any prior criminal arrests or convictions, so that should weigh in his favor." He shook his head. "I will say this: we need to get him out of there ASAP. He looked like a suicide risk."

"What?" Dante gasped. Even Sebastian looked unnerved.

"Let's just say that I'm glad they took his belt and shoelaces."

"What kind of bail are we looking at?" Jonathan asked. "Ballpark figure."

Sebastian shrugged. "Depends on how much they caught him holding. For a first-time offender in possession of a Schedule II drug like cocaine, the maximum fine is $2 million dollars, or a $200,000 bail, for five keys or less. If more than that, you're looking at $4 million dollars max, or a $400,000 bail." He looked over at Alex.

"I'd suggest planning for the higher end." Alex drank more beer.

Dante's stout stopped midway to his mouth in shock. "He was holding more than five keys?"

"I can't tell you that."

"Shite." Jonathan frowned and crossed his arms across his chest. His biceps, clearly visible in the tank top he wore, flexed beneath the multiple, colorful tattoos on each upper arm. "Nigel's always been a bit of a nancy. I can't see him trafficking that much cocaine."

"Who's got that kind of money?" Dante mused. "I'm just a lowly PhD, with not much to speak of."

Sebastian snorted. "You own your own businesses."

"And after paying myself and my employees, any extra goes back into the businesses, especially my research and development." Neither of them mentioned Dante's alternative yet lucrative revenue stream, which only he and Sebastian knew about, and which was the cause of friction in their relationship.

"Well, Uncle Joseph and Aunt Lisa's money is tied up in their rental properties in DC," Sebastian thought aloud. "They could feasibly put one or two up for collateral, but there are tenants inside; that may not sit well with the court."

"I'm surprised they have anything," Dante commented. "They're always bailing out their kids, including Nigel."

"I know no one's looking at me for money," Sebastian added. "I work for the government."

"Yes, we know that everyone makes more money than you and Tia," Alex teased. "Y'all are the underachieving twigs of the family tree."

Sebastian grinned. "But I get good benefits, though."

Alex made a talking motion with his hand. "Yeah yeah yeah, blah blah blah."

"Well, you blokes know that there is no real love lost between my mother and her siblings--at least on my mother's part--but she did a number on me much as Aunt Janelle did on Sebastian this evening. She gets along with Uncle Joseph more than the others, except for Uncle Brandon, so," Jonathan sighed as he ran a hand over his close-cropped hair, "I'll be putting up Nigel's bail."

Everyone gaped at Jonathan. "Seriously?" Dante asked.

Jonathan shrugged. "I'm the only one, other than Papa Pierre, who is liquid enough to make the payment. And no one is going to ask our grandparents for money, even though they'll offer."

"Wow." Silence fell as everyone digested his comment.

"We know you have it, Moneybags," Dante commented with a wicked grin. "Stocks, bonds, an Aston Martin, a Lotus Elise 111S, a Bentley Arnage, that huge house in London, and the chalet in Switzerland."

Jonathan flipped his middle finger at his cousin, causing the tattoo of currency symbols to dance in the overhead kitchen light. His career as an investment banker specializing in international business had been very good to him. "Whatever money I do or don't have, what makes you think I want to spend it on Nigel?" Everyone in the kitchen laughed.

Alex chuckled. "Regardless, you'd better find a sterling silver mine, Jon, and start digging. 'Cause you're gonna need all them pounds."

"My word. Have you always been this corny?" Jonathan was three years younger than Sebastian and Alex, but had been only two years behind them at Yale University, due to the superiority of the British educational system.

"I wasn't corny when I kicked your ass on line," Alex retorted. He had overseen Jonathan's pledge group during its initiation into Alex and Sebastian's fraternity. "And don't think I won't do it again."

"Yeah yeah yeah, blah blah blah." Jonathan mimicked Alex's talking-hand gesture.

"Well, we'll see how much the banks across the pond will cooperate when they open in," Jonathan checked his Tissot watch, "six hours. There's a five-hour time difference between here and London."

"You're getting the money wired?" Alex asked.

"Not from London to here; there are a few branches of Barclay here in New York, so I can simply stop in the nearest one. I'll have the funds wired from my account into Uncle Joseph's, so that they can withdraw it in U.S. certified funds. I'm sure the jail won't take personal checks or credit cards."

"Too bad that Nigel isn't old enough to come into his trust," Dante mused. All of the Pierre children and grandchildren had trust funds established for them by Nana and Papa. The kicker was that the principal could not be touched until the age of thirty-three; in the meantime, the interest payments were not bad at all. Sebastian, who had just turned 32 the previous month, would be coming into his principal next year, as would Dante three months later.

"Yeah, Nigel mentioned something about a trust fund," Alex said, "but he said he wouldn't come into it until he was thirty-three."

"He won't come into the principal," Jonathan corrected. "But he still gets interest payments. Not enough to make bail," he added at the interest in Alex's eyes.

67

"What does he do with the interest?" Sebastian inquired. He knew that he, his sister, and most of the cousins invested theirs, or had it invested for them if they were underage. Sebastian usually let Jonathan handle his investments. Not that Sebastian really cared what Nigel did with his money, outside of it impacting his drug charge.

Dante shrugged. "Hell if I know. But you know that Priscilla doesn't work outside the home, and he has those two little ones to feed, plus pay the rent and whatever other bills he has."

"But he's works in investment banking," Alex argued. "He should be pulling down a nice chunk of change, especially in New York."

"He's at a small, private investment firm," Jonathan replied. "While Quasar does make a tidy profit and has performed some high-profile deals by industry standards, it's still a small firm. Nigel's not making the money that he would at a larger, more established firm like Merrill Lynch or Goldman Sachs. Quasar just doesn't have the clientele or the cachet."

Alex started to make further comment but refrained as Priscilla entered the kitchen. She and the children had stayed the night, at Janelle's insistence.

"Hey, Pris," Dante said. "How are you feeling?"

"Fine," Priscilla replied, her voice shaded with weariness. She shuffled into the kitchen, pulling Tia's light blue terry cloth robe tighter about her slim body. Her brown eyes were red-rimmed and had heavy shadows beneath them. Her straight, dark hair had been pulled back into a haphazard ponytail at the nape of her neck, and was disheveled from tossing and turning. Nigel's arrest and imprisonment had taken a very hard toll on her. Especially since it was partially her fault. But what choice did she have? What choice did she really have?

"Sit down, Pris, there's a love," Jonathan murmured as he rose and offered her his chair. Priscilla sank into the chair and slumped against the back of it. She sniffled and wiped her nose with the sleeve of her robe.

"Want some coffee, Pris?" Sebastian asked. At her nod he turned and pulled coffee grounds and filters from a nearby cabinet. Soon the kitchen filled with the aroma of freshly brewed coffee.

"You hungry?" Dante asked. Not waiting for an answer, and not used to dealing with distraught women, Dante opened the refrigerator and pulled out foil- and plastic-covered dishes and bowls. "Uh, we got some roti left over, and some pelau. Oh, there's some shark and bake, too--how did I miss that earlier?" He shook his head in dismay. "What do you want?"

Priscilla sat in silence. Part of her was distraught over what her husband was going through. The other part of her was angry at the discussion she'd overheard the cousins having about Nigel. She pressed her lips tighter together for fear that she would explode from all the emotions that were warring within her. Her head pounded in response.

"Give her some roti, man," Alex instructed.

"Yeah, roti would be good right about now," Dante said nervously. Priscilla was never one to talk much, but her silence now was just eerie. For reasons none of the cousins could understand, she seemed to love Nigel. Dante heated a plate of the roti in the microwave and placed the steaming hot plate of food in front of Priscilla, along with a cup of freshly brewed coffee, creamer and sugar. The men all stood around uncomfortably, not knowing what to say. Priscilla took a bite of roti and placed her fork down.

"What's wrong? It's not hot enough?" Sebastian inquired.

"Do you want something else?" Dante asked.

"What can we do for you, Pris?" Jonathan questioned.

"Nothing," Priscilla choked out. "You've done enough."

The anger in her voice surprised the men in the room. They looked at each other then back at Pris. Jonathan spoke first. "Pris? What's wrong?"

She knew she had to play the role of the distraught wife, despite her plan. Priscilla injected more ire into her voice. "I know how much you don't like Nigel. I know you don't want to help him, help us." The words poured out in a torrent that Priscilla could not stop, even if she'd wanted to. "He hasn't done anything to you, but still you treat him poorly. If it's such a problem, then my husband and I will find another source of help." Her small fists remained clenched in her lap and her chest heaved as if she'd run a minute mile.

Guilt flashed across the faces of the Pierre cousins and Alex. Priscilla saw it and suppressed a smile at her ace performance. They all looked at each other again as Jonathan, in his adopted role as peacemaker, stooped and put his arm around Priscilla.

"Pris, we are family and we will help Nigel the best we can. Granted, we've had our differences in the past, and are not particularly close now. But we are all here for you both." Jonathan looked at the others and gave them significant looks.

Sebastian caught the hint. "I agree with Jonathan. We will help Nigel get to the bottom of this. I'm sure there was a mistake."

"Yeah," Dante concurred. "Nigel will be okay. You watch."

Alex was his usual blunt self. "We will all do what we can, Priscilla, regardless of our feelings for Nigel." Priscilla glared at Alex, who shrugged. "I'm just keeping it real."

FIVE

Trey Jacobson nursed a snifter of brandy as he relaxed in the private dining room of a small yet exclusive Italian restaurant. Opposite him, Simon Saldana dipped the tip of a Macanudo cigar into his own snifter. He held a match to the end and puffed until it glowed. "Let me see if I understand this correctly," Simon said. He stared at the smoke wafting from his cigar. "I sign paperwork that says that NTJ Holdings, a subsidiary of Quasar Financial, is willing to enter a loan swap agreement with Dalsana Holdings for one of my buildings downtown." Simon, under the auspices of Dalsana Holdings, also owned four other valuable properties in Manhattan and a string of dry cleaners. "I will pay NTJ 15% of the loan principal of $3 million dollars, which is fixed for five years. How did you come to a 15% rate, again?"

"The 15% is a combination of your 7.5% fixed interest rate, the LIBOR plus 3.5%, plus the 4% transactional fee." Trey sipped his brandy, relishing the smooth burn as it crawled down his throat to glow pleasantly in his belly.

Simon nodded. "Okay. So Dalsana pays NTJ 15% on a specified day of each month. NTJ, in return, pays Dalsana the difference between our fixed rate of 7.5% and the variable rate. You pay us more if the rate drops, and less if the rate rises. This continues for the period of the loan, which is five years, or until we cancel prior to the payment date, whichever comes first."

"Correct," Trey nodded. "We would require thirty days' notice prior to the next payment date if you wish to unravel this swap."

"I understand," Simon nodded. The subdued lighting gave his pale blonde hair an otherworldly glow. "And all of this is on paper, since Dalsana has no outstanding loans on my properties and therefore no interest in the interest rates, rising or otherwise. Payment will be made in kilograms of Blizzard, which you will distribute among Wall Street clientele. You will take the money from those transactions and note them as payments we are allegedly making on the swap, and apply them toward the swap criteria. When you have to pay us during loan rate drops, this money will serve as the source of payments that will go back into our not-so-legitimate enterprises. This will continue for six months, at which time we will cancel our swap. We will then withdraw the remainder of the money, which is now clean, and apply it to other areas within my empire."

"That's about it."

Simon grunted as he puffed on his cigar. Trey tried to hide his excitement as the server brought over small, leather-bound dessert menus. As he tried to decide between tiramisu and homemade gelato floated over a pony of Strega, he couldn't help but recall the journey he'd taken to this point. This was the third such deal that Trey had brokered. He had stumbled across the idea during a staff meeting over six months ago, and he had his dad to thank for it.

Quasar specialized in derivative-based transactions. Companies needed loan swaps in order to gain more favorable loan numbers. Trey initiated the loan swaps on paper, but actual payment was made with product and the interest gained became clean money. Everybody went home happy, provided that the payments are made on time. Better yet, if either company is not pleased with the other's performance, it could back out of the deal with thirty days' notice of doing so. Best of all, such a practice was perfectly legal. Trey simply saw a way to use a legal way of boosting revenue to solve some of the problems of businessmen with alternative streams of revenue, and boost his own revenue stream in the process.

Dealing Blizzard underneath his dad's nose just added frosting to the cake. Drug dealing embezzlement and fraud: just a little payback for dad talking about taking the company public, and feeling out potential buyers. Trey stuck his head deep into the snifter and inhaled the aroma of the brandy to calm down. The thought that his father would sell *his* inheritance, *his* future income, without so much as thinking of Trey's future was infuriating. After all Trey had done for that company; his father didn't realize how irritating it was working there, and having people think that Trey's successes were due to the fact that this father owned the company. Although Trey did admit to himself that he wouldn't have had anywhere near the same perks and leeway if he'd worked at a larger, more prestigious firm; he had to thank the old man for that. Things could be worse: he could have tried to give the company to Malcolm. Trey snorted as he stared at the menu with unseeing eyes. The way he had the deals set up, by the time Nate found out about them, it would be too late and Quasar would not look so attractive to investors, which would send said investors running in the opposite direction.

As if reading his mind, Simon said, "There are rumors that Quasar is about to do an initial public offering of stock."

Trey laughed it off, even as his insides twitched. "Rumors are always running rampant."

Simon stared at Trey with guileless, pale blue eyes. "My sources say that this is no rumor. That, in fact, they have met with your father with regard to pricing and control issues."

Trey took a healthy gulp of brandy. "Well, my father is just trying to test the waters. If there were to truly be an IPO, I'd be one of the first to know."

"Is that right?" Simon murmured as he puffed his cigar. "If you say so. I'd hate for rumor to become fact."

Trey didn't like the menacing tone in Simon's voice. He picked up the menu. "So, Simon, have you ever had their tiramisu? It's sinful."

SIX

Sebastian took his usual five-mile jog the next morning. He needed the release; the family was going to support Nigel at his magistrate hearing in a few hours, and the stress level would be even more elevated than it was now. His path took him around the neighborhood, where he could see the obvious effects of gentrification. He passed Stuman's Bakery, where his father used to get pastries for the family every Sunday, and where Sebastian used to stop for cake every Friday, when he received his allowance. As he jogged through Bed-Stuy, he had a wave of nostalgia; in some ways, he missed home. He had missed out on a lot of family milestones living on the west coast and while it had been a good start for his career with the Administration, maybe it was time to test what he'd learned in another place.

Sebastian had to admit to himself that since his shooting last year, he'd had an unspoken desire to be geographically closer to his parents. Then again, he liked California. He liked the weather, the women, the cases he'd been involved in. Then there were his friends, such as Zachary Demps, a Narcotics detective with the San Francisco Police Department, and Robert, his Group Supervisor at work; and Alex was only a few hours south in L.A. But Alex was always one for traveling, so it wasn't like they wouldn't see each other ever again. Zachary had mentioned that he was thinking of moving out of the SFPD, and maybe even California, and who knew where he would end up.

However, Sebastian couldn't really see himself moving back to New York. It would always be home for him, but the adult Sebastian no longer fit here. Plus, if he was to fulfill his dream of running his own field office as the Special Agent in Charge, he would have to move to Washington, DC, if he was to move anywhere. Within the Administration, all roads to a supervisory position of that nature led to DC. But that was all something to think about on another day. Right now, he had to get through this Nigel debacle and attempt to salvage at least some of his vacation.

Sebastian returned home to find his grandmother in the kitchen. "Hey Nana," he exclaimed with surprise before kissing her on the cheek. "What are you doing up so early?" He looked at the clock on the stove: it read 7:02 a.m.

"I'm helping your mother with breakfast," Nana Pierre replied as she grinned at her grandson, her grey eyes crinkling at the corners. She turned and picked up a large can of chickpeas, her long, thick, silver braid swinging behind her back. "The rest of the family will be here shortly. We're going to meet here before going over to the courthouse."

Sebastian nodded. Some of the family was going as a show of support for Nigel. His grandparents and the younger children were staying behind. Oscar, the eldest Pierre child, and his family were expected in later that day from California, and someone needed to be at the house for their arrival. "Where's Papa?"

"Downstairs with your father. They're doing something in that workshop of his."

Sebastian moved to the other side of his grandmother and kissed his mother on the cheek. "Morning, Mom."

Janelle wrinkled her nose at his sweaty, rumpled appearance. "Good morning. "

"What?" Sebastian made a show of sniffing underneath his arms. "Do I smell?"

"Don't you always?" Tia commented as she entered the kitchen in a green Garfield nightshirt over a pair of sweatpants.

"Just like your breath," Sebastian retorted. Tia took a swing at him in response and the siblings began to mock-box until Janelle put a stop to it.

"Enough of that roughhousing," she ordered as Tia bumped against the table. "This is a kitchen, not a playground. You take your antics into the other room. As a matter of fact, you need to get dressed; we'll be leaving for the courthouse shortly."

"Yes, Mom," Tia and Sebastian answered in unison. Sebastian took one last look at the table before they left the kitchen. He took in the cans of chickpeas; bags of flour; bottles of curry powder, coriander, cumin; cloves of garlic. "You're making doubles, Nana?" he asked in an excited voice. His grandmother's doubles were the best.

"You always did like my doubles. I never saw a little boy put away so many." Nana Pierre pushed up a sleeve of her blue velour tracksuit and removed a damp towel that covered a bowl of risen bara dough. She gave the dough a firm punch with her small fist, the gold bracelets on her slim wrist jingling with the effort. Her movements showed no trace of the stroke she'd suffered earlier that year. The dough deflated and she replaced the towel over it. "I thought it would be nice for the family to eat breakfast together, especially with all of this Nigel business." She poured some oil into a skillet and turned on the gas flame. Janelle, meanwhile, had been spooning a mixture of chickpeas and spices onto small rounds of prepared dough, then folding them in half. Nana dropped each completed mini-sandwich into the hot oil, the heat of it releasing the delicious aromas.

Sebastian hurried upstairs to shower and get dressed; he wanted to get a jump on the food before the rest of the family arrived. He pounded on the door to the bathroom between his and Tia's old bedrooms as he passed; he figured that either Jonathan or Dante was in there, as his father and mother had their own bathroom in the master suite. Alex had left early in order to visit Nigel; and Tia had more than likely commandeered his parents' bathroom, since it was bigger and more modern. "Hurry up! I need to get in there, too" he called.

"You slow, you blow!" a faint voice responded.

After a hasty lukewarm shower -- since whoever had been in there had hogged most of the hot water -- Sebastian dressed in simple khaki pants, a royal blue long-sleeved golf shirt, and loafers. He reached into his travel kit for his blue-and-gold enameled DEA badge and stared at it before sticking it, and his other credentials, in his pocket. While he carried it around out of habit, he never figured that he would actually need to use it while he was in New York. He'd thought about bringing Trixie, his beloved M9 Beretta, to New York with him, but his mother would kill him for bringing a gun into her house, legally or not. Plus, he would have had to check his bag, and he avoided doing that whenever possible.

Sebastian bounded downstairs and immediately started heaping a plate high with freshly cooked doubles. "Save some for the others," Nana laughed as she slapped the back of his hand while reaching for yet another. Soon, other members of the Pierre family filled the kitchen and scarfed down the hastily replenished food.

A commotion in the hallway presaged the entrance of a slim, gray-eyed older man with brown skin. "Hello, all," Oscar Pierre stated. His pressed khakis and long-sleeved red polo shirt showed no evidence of his red-eye flight from California. Right behind him was his wife, Juliette Barton Pierre, carrying their four year-old daughter, Grace. Oscar found himself a father for the first time after his second marriage to Juliette, who was fifteen years younger.

"Oscar!" Nana Pierre rushed over to hug and kiss her firstborn.

"Hello, Mummy," Oscar murmured as he enveloped his mother into a bear hug, lifting her off the ground. "Hello, Janelle, Michelle, Victoria, Reginald, Morris." He nodded in turn to each of his siblings and their respective spouses. He looked over at Jonathan with raised eyebrows. "Jonathan? Is that you, man? My God, you've grown up! It's been what, four years since I've seen you last?"

"Three, Uncle Oscar. I was in California for a conference a few years ago, and had dinner at your house."

"The bank must be treating you well."

"It's a job," Jonathan replied with a grin.

"And Dante! How have you been?"

Dante smiled. "I've been good, Uncle Oscar."

"We could use your top-notch brain over at the hospital," Oscar commented. He was a cardiologist at Stanford Medical Center and had been trying to lure Dante back into research since the latter's move to California two years ago. "Or, if you'd rather, the university is looking for some biochemists to teach some graduate courses."

"Thanks, Uncle Oscar, but Warner Environmental is doing well."

Oscar shrugged. "Oh well, can't blame me for trying." He turned his attention to the food on the table. "Mum, did you make doubles?" He walked over and retrieved a plate from the stack, piling it high with the snack-sized sandwiches.

"Sebastian almost ate them all, so be grateful you got here in time," Nana teased with a wink at her grandson.

"Dante, you haven't been by to visit in quite some time," Juliette scolded. "You either, Sebastian." She was as tall as Oscar, with a deep, melodious voice that held hints of her Toronto, Canada upbringing as the child of parents from Barbados. She wore her hair shorn close to her scalp, which only served to emphasize her feminine features. "I have some promising medical students that you two should meet."

"Sorry, Aunt Juli," Sebastian and Dante answered in unison. The men looked at each other sheepishly. They both avoided going to visit Juliette and Oscar due to her incessant matchmaking attempts. She, like their mothers, didn't understand why both men were still single and childless. And she might be a top-notch reproductive endocrinologist, but she couldn't boil water without burning it. Thank God they had a cook, even though Juliette unfortunately insisted on cooking for family and friends whenever they visited.

"'Bastian! 'Bastian!" Gracie struggled to get out of her mother's arms, reaching for Sebastian.

Sebastian took Gracie from her mom. "Hey, pretty girl!" He gave her a big kiss on her cheek as he balanced her weight on his hip. "How's my big girl doing?" Despite the almost thirty-year age difference, Sebastian and Gracie got along very well. Sebastian would pick her up and spend time with her as his schedule allowed. Gracie was often mistaken for his daughter, which garnered Sebastian a lot of female attention in public.

"I went to school," Gracie said with pride. Her gray eyes and long lashes were identical to Sebastian's. Her thick, dark brown hair was pulled to the top of her head in a single ponytail and adorned with yellow ribbons and bows to match her yellow, long-sleeved shirt and blue denim overalls. "And I got to paint."

"You did? What did you paint?"

"Gracie started a Montessori school," Juliette explained. "Half-days. I can work in the morning and be with her in the afternoon." The doctors Pierre were both in private practice.

Gracie turned and saw Dante. "'Tay! 'Tay!" She reached for Dante much as she had for Sebastian minutes earlier, and Sebastian handed her off. Dante and Jonathan, who stood near him and didn't get to see Gracie that often, played with their baby cousin.

"We weren't expecting you until later," Janelle commented as she walked over to hug her big brother. Michelle followed suit.

"We weren't planning to fly in until this afternoon," Oscar said as he placed his empty plate on the sideboard before draping an arm across the shoulders of each twin. "But when you called yesterday about this Nigel nonsense, we decided to come in straightaway."

Joseph and Brandon Pierre entered the kitchen, followed by Stephen and Papa Pierre. "Hello, everyone," Brandon said. "Oscar! You made it!" The youngest Pierre child hugged the eldest before placing a kiss on Juliette's cheek. Heather Pierre, Brandon's youngest child, trailed behind and made a beeline for Jonathan. She enveloped him in a big hug.

"Hi Jonathan," the sixteen year-old Heather smiled, showing her braces. Her gray eyes glowed with the crush she'd had on her glamorous British cousin for years.

"Hiya, Heather, love," Jonathan said as he returned the hug. Regina and his Aunt Michelle had made him aware of Heather's crush, so he made an extra effort to pay her attention without encouraging her.

"Harrison couldn't make it?" Oscar asked Brandon.

"He had already agreed to cover someone's shifts this weekend, but he was going to try and get up here sometime this weekend, or definitely next week, before Mom and Dad return to Trinidad." Harrison, Brandon's eldest son, was an emergency medicine doctor in Philadelphia.

"I hate to break up this Hallmark moment," Dante said as he looked at his watch, "but you guys have to get a move on if you're going to make it to court in time."

"What do you mean, 'you guys'?" Tia asked. "You're going with us, right?"

Dante shook his head with a sheepish expression. "I can't take seeing Nigel in prison gear. I'll just wait here at the house."

Chairs and bodies shuffled as everyone rose to leave the kitchen. Some grabbed food to take with them. Soon everyone that was going to the courthouse piled out of the house and into cars. Sebastian drove and, Tia, Regina and Jonathan rode with him.

Sebastian led the convoy to the Daniel Patrick Moynihan United States Courthouse on Pearl Street in Manhattan. After securing paid parking, the Pierres began the tedious process of being cleared through security. Sebastian got through a bit faster than the others, due to being law enforcement. They all convened in courtroom number four, where Nigel was to be arraigned.

Sebastian was not unfamiliar with a courtroom, having had to testify in drug cases. His relatives, however, were not as comfortable and looked around with wide eyes at their surroundings. They noticed the twin flags of the US Federal District Court and of the United States of America against the heavy wood paneling and brass fixtures They took in the empty judge's bench; the empty jury box; the court reporter who sat with her hands poised over her stenography machine; the guards who were stationed around the perimeter of the room, hands ready on their guns. Sebastian fixed his eyes on two men, whom he pegged to be the DEA agents on this case. One was an Asian man in a blue shirt and dark tie, the other was a Latino man wearing a white shirt and brown patterned tie, with his badge hanging about his neck from a chain.

The bailiff entered the room from the rear. "All rise," he ordered. Everyone in the room stood. "The Honorable Anna Maxwell Gregson presiding."

Judge Gregson strode to the bench, her black robes swirling about a painfully thin body. Her hair was silver and blonde and scraped back from her face, calling attention to the many lines and crags that covered it. A slash of dark orange lipstick and two red rounds on her cheekbones were the only color in an otherwise pale pallor.

Alex sat in the front row of the courtroom, along with other attorneys. A prison guard entered with a line of fifteen prisoners, all wearing handcuffs and ankle shackles. The shackles were strung together with a heavy-duty chain to further minimize escape. The men sat in a row, forming a bright orange wall. The backs of their jumpsuits were emblazoned with "NYDC" in large black letters. Lisa Pierre began to cry at the sight of her firstborn in shackles. Nigel looked rough, as one would expect after almost twenty-four hours in jail. He had heavy beard stubble on his jaw and his hair was unkempt. His gray eyes drooped from lack of sleep and were red-rimmed from crying. The baggy jumpsuit was close to falling off his naturally thin frame.

The Pierres sat through three cases before Nigel's was called. Lisa Pierre became more nervous with each passing case; her lap was littered with shreds of facial tissue. Judge Gregson seemed to be a hanging judge; she had denied bail for each of those three cases, delivering her decision with precise diction and a cold blue stare. Then again, each of those men was a repeat offender who had been in the drug game for years. Perhaps Nigel would fare better.

"Docket number 04FMC0523, the Government of the United States of America versus Nigel Pierre," the bailiff intoned. A guard unlocked the group chain from Nigel's ankles and led him to the defense bench. Alex sat there, making notes on a legal pad and reviewing what additional paperwork he had been able to obtain. He was dressed in a navy blue Armani suit with a faint chalk pinstripe and a crisp white shirt, his silk tie and matching handkerchief appropriately somber in shades of navy blue and gray. The stainless steel bracelet of his Tissot watch peeked bashfully from beneath his French cuffs, in which he wore his favorite fraternity crest cufflinks. He had trimmed his goatee and mustache and looked every inch the successful attorney that he was. He rose as Nigel was steered beside him.

The Assistant U.S. Attorney, Jordan Stavros, was a short, tanned man with a beaked nose and heavy black eyebrows that provided a dramatic contrast to his halo of silver hair. His tailored charcoal gray suit caressed his cement-block body lovingly and was offset by a bright red tie and matching handkerchief.

Judge Gregson perused the paperwork before her. "Mr. Pierre, you have been charged with possession of eight kilograms of a designer cocaine blend, street name Blizzard, with the intent to distribute. How do you plead?"

Sebastian blinked in surprise. Nigel had been busted with Blizzard?

Nigel looked at Alex, who nodded. "Not guilty, Your Honor."

"Your Honor," Stavros rose. "The people wish to deny bail to the defendant on the grounds that he is a flight risk."

"Your Honor, my client fits none of the characteristics of a flight risk, and this is his first criminal offense," Alex argued.

Stavros smoothed his hand over his coiffed hair. His voice was harsh with a faint undercurrent of his parents' native Cyprus. "Your Honor, the defendant has ties to the countries of Trinidad and Tobago, as well as Canada and the United Kingdom. He has extended family there and may seek asylum in order to avoid prosecution."

Alex glared at Stavros, even as he wondered how Stavros dug up Nigel's family ties so quickly. "Your Honor, while my client does have family ties to the Republic of Trinidad and Tobago, as well as Canada and the United Kingdom, it is worth noting that his entire family is in New York for a family reunion;

therefore there is no reason for him to leave the country."

Stavros returned Alex's glare before trying another tack. "Even if that is true, Your Honor, the fact that the defendant has access to residence in other countries, and has resources for survival, is more than enough reason to deny bail."

Alex shook his head. "With all due respect, Your Honor, it seems that the prosecution is implying that the aforementioned countries, all of which enjoy an excellent relationship with the United States that includes prompt extradition of known criminals when necessary, would willingly harbor a U.S. fugitive. This is, of course, contingent upon my client having the faulty judgment to attempt the flee the country with federal charges against him."

"Enough," Judge Gregson ordered. She looked at Nigel, tapping her pen against her thin lips, measuring. She looked back over the paperwork and made her decision. "Your request is denied, Mr. Stavros, as the defendant is a first-time offender and his family origins have no bearing upon this court. However, due to the quantity of Blizzard found in his possession, I will revoke his passport until the conclusion of the trial and ask that he remain within the state of New York. Bail is set at $4 million dollars." She banged her gavel, bringing an end to the arraignment. "Next case."

Sebastian's eyes closed. Eight keys of Blizzard, with a $4 million bail. What the hell did Nigel get himself into? He opened his eyes to see Alex leaving the defense bench, and then the courtroom. He looked at Jonathan and jerked his head in Alex's direction. Jonathan rose and followed to post Nigel's bail.

~~~

Two hours later, a subdued Nigel rode back with his parents to the Scott home. While Nana plied Nigel with food, Sebastian pulled Alex aside.

"Alex, is there any way that I can see your copy of Nigel's arrest report?"

"Yeah, no problem. Nigel had already given me permission to discuss his case with you; I forgot to mention it last night." He looked at his friend curiously. "Why? What's up?"

"Nigel got busted with Blizzard, instead of regular cocaine."

"Yeah. So?"

"I just busted a mid-level dealer on a buy of twenty keys of Blizzard, right before I came out here. It's arrogant of me to assume that Blizzard was only on the west coast, but still, it's surprising that it would turn up now."

"The timing is interesting," Alex conceded, "But it could be just a coincidence. You think the two cases are connected?"

"Not really, but I don't believe in coincidence." Sebastian stared in the distance as he planned his next steps. "I'll need to do some back-channel digging, since I can't ask about Nigel's case outright."

"Alright. I'll get you that paperwork, as soon as I get out of this suit." Alex clapped Sebastian on the shoulder as he loosened his tie and went upstairs.

Sebastian pulled out his phone, calculated the time difference, and made a call.

"This is Zachary," a groggy voice answered.

"What's up, man?"

"Sebastian?" Zachary turned over and stared at his alarm clock with a bleary brown eye. "Dude, what time is it?

"My bad if I woke you up. I was expecting to leave a voicemail."

"I just finished pulling a double shift because we're short-staffed. A lot of folks have been calling out with the Blue Flu to protest our new police chief. So I'm exhausted." He yawned. "So why are you calling me at," he did some mental calculations, "twelve-fourteen in the afternoon, your time? I take it this is not a social call?"

"I wish it was, man. I was calling about that Blizzard case the DEA closed before I left.

"Yeah, I heard about that. Some of the guys in my unit were in on the bust."

"I wanted to know if you'd heard anything else about it; namely, what is moving out here on the east coast."

Zachary adjusted the pillow beneath his head. "You know, Sebastian, the term 'vacation' implies that one does not think about work at all, except maybe in passing, such as 'Man, I'm glad I'm not at work.'"

"Believe me, I wish I didn't have to."

Zachary caught the bitterness in his friend's tone. He sat up and reached for the pack of cigarettes on his nightstand. "What's going on, man?"

Sebastian gave Zachary a brief rundown on the Nigel situation. Zachary pondered as he took a drag of his cigarette.

"You know I don't believe in coincidence, so there is a definite possibility that the two cases are connected. I can reach out to the brothers out your way, see what I can find out. You know that they would cream at the thought of knowing something that the Feds don't."

"Hah."

"Anyway, I'm sorry to hear about your cousin. Sounds like your vacation just got all fucked up."

"Basically."

"Well, I'm going back to sleep. I'll be in touch when I get something to be in touch about."

"I don't mean to rush you, but I'm only going to be here for a few more days."

"I'll get on it as soon as I wake up, then."

"'Preciate it, man."

"Don't mention it."

Sebastian turned the phone over in his hands as he contemplated another resource; one that was downstairs with the rest of their family. One that he really didn't like to think about. He trudged back downstairs and signaled to Dante, who was in the kitchen again.

Dante brought along a hunk of rum cake on a napkin. "What's up?" he asked as Sebastian pulled him into his father's empty den.

"I need your help."

Dante popped a chunk of cake into his mouth and chewed slowly, all the while staring at Sebastian. "You need my help?" he asked after swallowing.

"Yeah."

"*You* need *my* help." Dante's grey eyes twinkled with amusement. "It's killing you to admit that, isn't it?"

It looked like Dante was going to make Sebastian pour his pride on the rocks and gulp it down. "Look, if it was anyone but Nigel..."

"Yeah, we wouldn't be having this conversation, or any conversation at all. I get it." He continued to stare at his estranged cousin. Finally, he sighed. "Go ahead. Ask your questions."

"Did you make it?"

"Make what?" At Sebastian's pointed look, Dante leaned back against his uncle's desk and crossed his feet at the ankles. "Oh, Blizzard. Nope; I try to stay away from opioid derivatives. Too much federal heat." He winked at Sebastian. "Plus, I'm a small-market kind of guy. I don't have the time nor inclination to make street quantities."

Sebastian's jaw clenched. "Do you know who did?"

Dante eyed Sebastian as he pinched off another piece of cake. "No. And before you ask, I operate on a need-to-know basis and right now, I have no need to know."

Sebastian blew out a frustrated breath. "Could you do it? Make it, I mean."

"There is very little that I can't make." Dante shrugged. "However, what I can or cannot do is irrelevant. It's not going to help find out who planted those drugs in Nigel's desk."

"But if it's a designer drug, and you say that you can make it, then it stands to reason that someone else can too. Someone who does deal in street-level quantities."

"Blizzard isn't hard to make," Dante admitted. "OxyContin, cocaine, Ritalin. Very commonly prescribed, and accessible, drugs. But to do kilograms, one would need a steady pipeline of all of the above. For OxyContin and Ritalin, I'd be checking DEA numbers of physicians who've been prescribing a bit too much for comfort. Maybe even psychiatrists who consult with public schools; plenty of Ritalin prescriptions there, especially in lower-income communities. For the coke, I'd definitely check Manhattan: Upper East Side, Wall Street, clubs. The one percent do love their pick-me-ups." He shifted his weight. "But that's a long-term thing to look into. The more pressing issue is who framed Nigel, and why. I figure if you can find that out, they'll tell you who the candy man is."

Sebastian nodded as he processed Dante's words. His brilliant, award-winning, published biochemist cousin knew what he was talking about; he'd built a successful, and extremely lucrative, shadow business creating and selling designer drugs. "Alright. Thanks, Dante."

"Don't mention it."

Alex returned with the paperwork from Nigel's case, and found Sebastian in the den. He plopped down on the creaky leather couch with a sigh of relief as Sebastian took the papers and sat at his father's desk. He quickly read through the arrest report and Alex's notes on his interview with Nigel.

Jonathan walked past the den, then backed up at the sight of Sebastian, Alex, and Dante in there. "There you are. Aunt Janelle is wondering where you'd gotten to""

"Just going through the paperwork on Nigel's case," Sebastian answered absently as he continued to read.

Jonathan sat in a leather chair adjacent to the couch. "What of it?"

Sebastian pinched the bridge of his nose. "It's a setup, and an obvious one at that." He tossed the papers on the desk. "Proving it, however, is going to be difficult."

"What's going to be difficult to prove?" Dante asked. "That Nigel did, or did not, do it?"

"So you don't think Nigel did it?" Jonathan asked.

"Please," Dante snorted. "Nigel couldn't find his ass with GPS and a flashlight, let alone eight kilograms of a designer cocaine mix."

"Don't be so bloody crass," Jonathan shot back with a smile.

Alex raised an eyebrow at Dante's comment. "How do you know that Blizzard is a designer drug?"

Dante shot a glance at Sebastian, then answered Alex. "I know. Plus, such a mixture of three separate drugs--two of them only available by prescription--doesn't occur in nature. Someone had to put them together."

"Is that hard to do?" Jonathan asked.

Dante shrugged. "Not if you know what you're doing."

Jonathan looked from Dante to Sebastian as they avoided looking at each other. "Why do I get the feeling that I'm missing something significant from this conversation?"

Alex also picked up on something unsaid between the two cousins, but decided to ask Sebastian about it privately.

"Anyway," Dante ignored Jonathan, "you really think Nigel is innocent?"

Sebastian nodded as he sipped his coffee. "As much as I'd like him out of my life, he didn't do this."

"But the police have evidence, and a lot of it," Jonathan argued. "Everything points to Nigel."

"Exactly," Sebastian agreed. "It's too perfect, especially if you know Nigel."

"True," Dante concurred. "Nigel doesn't have the ambition or the organization to carry off distributing drugs. Eight keys is significant weight to be moving, and Nigel can't even open the childproof cap on a bottle of aspirin." He looked at Alex. "What's up with his legal counsel?"

"I have some leads, but no one has committed yet. So, right now, I'm still it."

"You sound real happy about that."

"Well...Nigel isn't the most difficult client I've ever had, but he's creeping into the top twenty." He looked over at Sebastian. "Now, I get it." Sebastian raised his coffee cup in acknowledgement.

Sebastian rubbed his hands across his face. "I need to talk to Nigel." He looked over at Alex.

"As his legal counsel, I'll have to be present."

"Fine with me."

"You want I should collect him? "Jonathan asked. He left at Sebastian's nod, and returned shortly with Nigel in tow. He shut the door to the den behind him.

Nigel still had a shell-shocked look from his foray into the wrong side of the judicial system. His grey eyes danced over Dante and Alex, then drilled Sebastian in suspicion. "Jonathan said you wanted to talk to me?"

"Yes. I have some questions about what happened before you were arrested."

"Okay." When Jonathan and Dante made to leave the room, Nigel stopped them. "No, you guys can stay. It's okay." The two men went back to their seats.

Sebastian pulled his phone out of his pocket and opened the voice recorder app. "I'm going to record this, so I can go over it later." He recited his name, date and time, and both Nigel and Alex's names. "Nigel, you work at Quasar Financial Services, correct?"

Nigel nodded. "Yes. I'm a Junior Financial Analyst."

"What do you do?"

"I review client contracts, set up client profiles, perform cost/benefit analyses, create financial projections, set up the initial portions of loan swaps. It's a lot of research and presentations, basically. I do whatever needs to be done, or whatever work the partners give me."

"Who has access to your cubicle, Nigel?"

"Everyone, I guess," Nigel said in a puzzled tone. "I mean, it's a cubicle; it's not like I have a door that I can lock. I'm not usually away from it for very long."

"Do you lock your desk up when you leave?"

Nigel shook his head. "No, unless I'm leaving for the day. There's really no need."

"Have any strange people been in your cubicle?"

Nigel raised an eyebrow. "I have clients coming into the office sometimes, but I don't know that you would consider them strangers, exactly. And I usually meet with them in one of the smaller conference rooms."

Sebastian felt a headache coming on. "I mean complete strangers, Nigel. Someone you wouldn't recognize, or had never seen before."

Nigel's brow furrowed. "Well, there was a new UPS man not too long ago."

"Did he come into your cubicle?"

"No. All packages are left with Assata, at the receptionist's desk. Then she distributes them."

Sebastian closed his eyes and took a deep breath, the better to keep from throttling Nigel. Had his cousin always been this dense? "Nigel," he said in a quiet tone, "how did that Blizzard get into your filing cabinets?"

"I don't know!" Nigel's face screwed up. He would not cry in front of his cousins. He would not give Sebastian or any of the others anymore reason to look at him with contempt. "I hardly use those drawers. Most of my files are within reaching distance. The last time I looked in those drawers was before I went to Miami."

"Why did you go to Miami?"

"I went because my job sent me there," Nigel said in an exasperated voice. "We were working on a loan swap with the Miami-Dade County waterworks department. Then we went back to work on the swap between the county and an Cuban-American art museum."

"When did you go?" Sebastian did not consciously realize it, but he had shifted into a familiar interrogation pattern. He was no longer Nigel's cousin; he was a cop. The transition made Nigel even more nervous, and was not lost on the other three men in the room, either.

"Two, three months ago. I was gone for a week."

"By yourself?"

Nigel's eyes narrowed. He was getting tired of all these questions. He just wanted to go home and go to sleep. "I went with a senior partner, who was the lead on that account."

"Name?"

"Malcolm Jennings. And what do my whereabouts have to do with anything?"

"Plenty, if you're innocent."

"You don't have to be so mean."

"Mean?" Sebastian looked at Nigel as if he'd lost his mind. "The prosecution will be even harder on you. You have to be prepared, Nigel." Alex nodded in agreement, but otherwise remained quiet.

"You're just loving this, aren't you?" Nigel snarled. "You love lording this over me."

"Lording what?"

"This whole arrest thing." Nigel glowered at Sebastian. "You always have to show off how smart and perfect you are."

Sebastian was fed up with Nigel, his situation, being dragged into it due to family pressure--all of it. "Nigel, I have no idea what you are talking about. But right now, my smarts are all that is standing between your freedom, and you becoming someone's bitch in a federal pen."

Nigel rose, fists clenched, and took two steps toward Sebastian. "I'm sick of taking your shit, Sebastian."

Sebastian straightened and balled his own fist. "If you're feeling froggy, then leap." The ice in his tone matched the chill in his eyes.

"Alright, you two," Alex warned. He bit back a smirk; though a fight between those two would be quite entertaining and long overdue, Sebastian would have mopped the floor with Nigel. "Cut it out. Nigel, Sebastian is only trying to help, which is what you wanted. And Sebastian, chill with the cop mode, a'ight?"

A knock on the door, then Priscilla entered with Miles on her hip. "I thought I heard you, Nigel." She looked at the other men and sensed the tension in the air. "What's going on in here?"

"I'm just trying to get some clarity on the timeline up until Nigel's arrest," Sebastian answered. Nigel downgraded his glower to a mere frown.

"Oh." She fought to keep the warring emotions of guilt and relief off her face as she buried her face in Miles's soft curls.

Sebastian's eyes narrowed at the shadow that had passed over Priscilla's face. If he didn't know better, he'd say that Priscilla looked guilty. He pushed that thought away. Priscilla? No, she couldn't possibly be mixed up in any of this; she was Nigel's wife, and didn't seem to be the deceptive type, not that he had reason to be around her much over the years. Still, Sebastian filed the impression away in the back of his mind.

SEVEN

Nate called an early morning meeting for his executive staff the day after the Nigel debacle. Nate sat behind his massive mahogany desk while Malcolm, Curtis Harris, Jeff, and Trey sat in front of him in a semicircle.

Nathaniel glowered at his senior and junior partners from sleep-deprived eyes. He had been wooing a potential client in Los Angeles when his executive assistant called to tell him of the DEA raid and Nigel's arrest. "Somebody want to explain to me why I had to potentially jeopardize this deal with Smithson Investments, because the fucking DEA was raiding my offices?" Nate had taken a red-eye flight back to New York, and had just arrived only an hour ago. His lack of sleep, combined with this fiasco, meant that he was on a short fuse. "What the fuck was the DEA doing here?"

Malcolm answered first, having cut short his own trip to Chicago the night before. "The DEA had a warrant for Nigel's arrest. They claimed that he had been trafficking some sort of special cocaine through this office."

"Tra...trafficking cocaine? Here? At Quasar?" With each sentence, Nate's voice rose higher. A large vein over his left temple began to throb violently. Malcolm watched it, fascinated.

"It's true," Trey piped up. "They caught him with some keys of cocaine and everything. He had them hidden in his filing cabinets." Right where Trey had them planted.

Nate was speechless. He figured that some of his employees did recreational drugs like marijuana, or maybe an occasional hit of something stronger; he wasn't naïve. But actually dealing drugs...it was a ludicrous concept, one that he would have never guessed in a million years. Now he had one employee in jail and going up on federal charges, a ton of existing clients to placate, and a lot of tap-dancing to do for future ones. "I shouldn't have to tell any of you that this couldn't have come at a worse time. We were, are," Nate corrected himself, "poised to start an initial public offering of stock next year." He sighed and removed a cigar from the wooden humidor on his desk, even though it was not even ten o'clock in the morning. He clipped the end, lit it, and took a deep drag. The fragrant smell of premium Cuban tobacco filled the room. "I'm ready to hear some ideas on damage control before I meet with our PR department, right after this."

"I think that Malcolm should be the one to handle this mess," Trey began. "After all, it's his fault that Nigel was hired in the first place."

Malcolm's look to Trey was anything but friendly. "How is his hiring my fault, when Nate makes the final decision?"

Trey scowled. "If I recall correctly, you were the one that pushed for Nigel to be hired, even though we had other, more qualified candidates. And, he's your mentee. Maybe we should be looking at you."

A dull flush worked into Malcolm's face. "And if I recall correctly, I acknowledged that there were other candidates who looked better on paper and did indeed have more experience in the areas of public and municipal finance. Plus, he was doing work for you while I was out of town." His tone was cool and did not reflect the anger pressing against his chest, or sparking in his dark brown eyes. "But unlike you, Trey, I look at the big picture.

"Nigel's family owns Pierre International, a rather lucrative condiment and cocoa exportation business that is based in Trinidad, but has offices in London and New York. His grandfather founded it, and still sits on the Board of Directors. Nigel is an heir to the family fortune, which is estimated to be somewhere around $4.5 billion dollars and includes vast real estate holdings worldwide. The company itself made $224 million dollars last year alone, and that was just based on the figures collected at the duty-free shops at the airports in both Trinidad and Tobago." Malcolm paused and trained his gaze on Nate. "That is a potential relationship that could translate into a significant cash flow for Quasar, especially if Pierre International could be encouraged to expand further in the United States." In his peripheral vision, Malcolm noted with satisfaction the embarrassed look on Trey's face. "So I stand by my previous recommendation."

"A foothold into the international market would boost our stock offering prices and would help Quasar establish itself as a legitimate overseas presence," Curtis added.

Trey rolled his eyes at Curtis. Did the man ever get tired of riding Malcolm's nut sack? "Not if this particular meal ticket is in jail." Out of the corner of his eye, he noticed that Jeff was slumped in his chair, chewing his nails while his eyes darted back and forth between the other three men. His knee jittered, which caused the keys in his pocket to jangle in syncopation.

A cold look from Nate caused Jeff to cease the nervous mannerism.

Curtis pursed his lips. "Whatever, Trey."

Nate puffed on the cigar to keep from cursing. He looked over at Trey and was once again disappointed in his only child. He never understood why Trey expressed so little interest in Quasar, except to pad his expense accounts and drive the flashy sports car that was part of his corporate benefits package for the executive staff. And his animosity towards Malcolm was puzzling. Malcolm had not done anything, to Nate's knowledge, to warrant it. He knew that the two men had crossed paths at Drexel University as undergraduates, but had never been friends. "I agree with Malcolm," Nate said after releasing another burst of fragrant smoke. "You have to look to the future, Trey. Everything is not always about instant gratification. But Trey also has a point; if Nigel is incarcerated, then this gamble will be moot." His gaze switched back to Malcolm. "Now, Malcolm, you worked closely with Nigel, did you not?"

Malcolm nodded. "For the most part. He was assigned as the financial analyst for the Miami-Dade County Waterworks project. He was good at research." He shrugged one shoulder. "His customer service skills could use some work; he was rather shy, but overall we had no complaints from the client. The deal went through smoothly and then we came home."

"Have you worked with him on anything else down there?"

Malcolm measured his tone. "I brought him in on the pitch for the Cubano-Americano Art Museum swap, which was also in Miami. He was very knowledgeable during the sales meeting. Then I put him on a plane for home to prepare the paperwork, while I stayed behind to tie up loose ends." Malcolm chose not to mention the after-hours negotiations he had personally conducted with Maribel Estéfan, the founder and curator of the museum.

Nate frowned. "The fact that Nigel is connected to Miami concerns me. It's a major drug conduit for most of the world." He studied the smoke that wafted from the cigar, which rested in the cut-glass ashtray on his desk. "How much cocaine did they find on him?"

Trey shrugged. "I don't know, but it's enough to bring him up on federal charges. So we're looking at least a few kilograms."

Malcolm looked at Trey with narrowed eyes. "You seem to know an awful lot about Nigel's case, especially since he just got arrested less than twenty-four hours ago."

"It pays to be informed." And it pays to pay to be informed. A small cash donation to one of the jail guards, who had told Trey what he needed to know: which was that, barring an eleventh-hour miracle, Nigel would not see the light of day for many years, if ever.

"Fine." Nate rested his tented fingers on his chin. "Trey, keep me informed of anything you discover regarding Nigel's charges. The rest of you figure out how we are going to spin this. I will tell you that we have a press conference scheduled for noon today. I want everyone there looking contrite and supportive. Yes," Nate shot Trey a warning look as he opened his mouth in protest, "supportive. The law says he's innocent until proven guilty, so let's apply that and show some solidarity. That's how we do things within the Quasar family."

Malcolm schooled his expression into a neutral one. The Quasar "family" was about as dysfunctional as they came, but if Nate chose not to see that, then Malcolm wasn't going to force him to do otherwise.

~ ~ ~

Nigel sat on the floor in the living room of their apartment, playing with Maya and Miles, enjoying the sense of calm such an activity brought him. It was amazing how he now appreciated the simple things, even something as insignificant as two-ply toilet paper. He looked over at Priscilla, who was sitting in their small beige-and-blue kitchen, nursing a cup of ginger tea. It had to have been cold by now, yet Priscilla continued to sip from it, staring out of the small kitchen window through which weak sunlight shone. She occasionally broke from her trance to wipe her nose; all of this legal stress had made her susceptible to a cold, she'd told him.

Priscilla was lost in her own thoughts. She mentally calculated the amount of money she had stashed away, which totaled to about $150,000. Enough to start over decently enough, somewhere else. She looked over at her children, roughhousing with her husband. As much as she tried, the new life she envisioned did not include them. Should Nigel go to prison, Priscilla figured that Nigel's parents would take care of Maya and Miles, and the rest of the family would pitch in.

"Everything alright, Pris?" Nigel asked.

Priscilla turned to look at her husband of over three years. She felt a slight stirring of pity, but that was about it. Had she ever loved him? "Everything's fine, Nigel," she replied with a wan smile.

Nigel stood and walked over to Priscilla, while Maya and Miles continued to play with building blocks. He began to massage her shoulders. The sunlight glinted off the plain gold wedding band on his left ring finger and Nigel frowned down at it. When they'd gotten engaged, he couldn't afford to buy Priscilla a nice engagement ring. He had a part-time job on campus, which didn't pay much; his scholarship took care of tuition, books, and room and board, but that was about it. Not wanting to look like a sucker, and wanting to hold on to the first woman who had shown him significant romantic attention, Nigel used the money from his trust fund interest and bought her a four-carat diamond ring. The look of amazement and adoration on her face was worth the money Nigel had spent.

Ever since then, Nigel had made it a point to spend his interest money on Priscilla and, when she got pregnant, the kids. While Nigel enjoyed the atmosphere at Quasar and liked working with Malcolm, he knew that he wouldn't make the money he needed to keep Priscilla in the lifestyle to which he'd like for her to become accustomed; indeed, he'd blown through the money he'd saved working for his grandfather. He tried to supplement his income with stock and real estate investments, but they never turned out as he wanted and he lost more money than he gained. A perverted sense of pride kept Nigel from consulting his cousin Jonathan, who probably could have invested his money and grown it more effectively. This meant that he had to occasionally ask his parents for money to help he and Priscilla pay bills. Of course, he told no one of these ventures; he didn't want anyone to think that he couldn't take care of his family. When his parents would inquire as to why he needed to borrow money, Nigel would tell them that he and Priscilla were saving to buy a house.

Nigel turned his attention back to Priscilla. Despite his ministrations, her shoulder muscles were still hard. "Things will work out, Priscilla. Sebastian is looking into things, and Alex is a good attorney."

Priscilla snorted. Nigel was so naïve. "Sebastian hates your guts and Alex does divorces."

Nigel raised his eyebrows. He'd never heard that bitter tone in her voice before. "Sebastian and I have had our differences, but I don't think that he would deliberately withhold help. And Alex is very intelligent; he does divorce work because he wants to, not because he has to. He said he'd find us someone who can help with criminal cases. He has some leads already."

"Yet and still, I wish your family wasn't involved."

Nigel removed his hands from Priscilla's shoulders and walked around to sit in the chair beside her. "What are you talking about, Pris? What happened? Did someone do or say something to you?" He placed his hand over hers, the cool surface of the diamonds scraping against the palm of his hand.

"Nothing." Priscilla sniffled and removed her hand from underneath his. "I'm just saying that everyone is in our business now. I don't like it." She wiped her nose with a paper napkin.

Nigel wiped a weary hand over his face. "I don't particularly like it, either, but right now we don't have much of a choice." He started to say something further but Miles was tugging on his pants leg.

"What's wrong, sport?" Nigel inquired. Miles continued to pull at his pants leg and started to cry. Nigel scooped the boy up in his arms and kissed his chubby cheeks. Maya toddled over, holding on to various inanimate objects as she made her way over to her father. Maya had her father's grey eyes and her mother's strong will. Miles was more easygoing, like Nigel, and was the spitting image of Priscilla with a high forehead, patrician nose, brown eyes and thinner lips.

Priscilla cast a disinterested glance over the children. "It's time for their nap. They're already late for it."

Nigel picked Maya up with his other arm and stood with both children. Between working later than he planned and the occasional business travel, he had no idea of his children's daily schedules. "Then I think it's time for a nap." He toted the children into their bedroom and placed Maya in the bottom bunk bed, and Miles in the crib. Maya reached out and grabbed at his leg as Nigel tried to leave.

"Stay, Daddy," Maya pouted.

Nigel looked over at Miles, who had already drifted off to sleep. "Okay, Princess." Nigel lay down beside his daughter, who smiled and buried her face into Nigel's chest. A deep wave of emotion almost choked Nigel as he looked down at her dark curls. He kissed her hair and inhaled the scent of baby lotion and innocence. Soon father and daughter were fast asleep.

Fifteen minutes later, Priscilla looked into the children's room and saw that they, along with Nigel, were asleep. Priscilla shook her head as she retraced her steps. She always had a hard time getting Miles and Maya to sleep, yet Nigel could do it in an instant. The children seemed to take to him so much better than to her, even though she was the one with them for most of the time. Maybe she wasn't cut out to be a mother. She partially closed the bedroom door.

Priscilla couldn't stand the silence in the house so she flipped channels on the television, turned on the radio, flipped through magazines. Nothing could quiet the anxiety in her mind and soul. She stared at her cell phone and bit her lip. Sighing, she dialed a preprogrammed number. A man's gruff voice answered. "Hello?"

"Hi, it's me."

"Me, who?"

"Priscilla."

"What?" The voice snapped in irritation.

"I need to come by."

"Now?"

"Yes."

"Fine."

"I'll be there shortly." The call disconnected.

Priscilla made one last check on Nigel and the kids and left a note, saying that she ran out to the store. As she walked down the busy streets of Brooklyn, she reflected upon her life to date. She adjusted her bright orange scarf against the evening chill.

Priscilla Carrington had left Antigua to attend Amherst College in Massachusetts. She'd won a full scholarship and was determined to put distance between herself and her impoverished upbringing. She wasn't worried about her family; her parents had died, and she and her siblings weren't close. During her sophomore year, she'd come across a nice-looking boy in the library. She had seen him in her English class, had noticed him staring at her when he thought she wasn't looking. She liked his kind, grey eyes and the way he would avert his gaze whenever she turned in his direction. One day, Priscilla walked over to him and asked to borrow his class notes. They exchanged phone numbers and within a month, Nigel Pierre and Priscilla Carrington were officially a couple.

Priscilla stared out the subway train window as she remembered how Nigel would court her. He would buy her flowers and take her out to dinner, even if it was just to a local sports bar. On her birthday, he took her to an expensive Italian restaurant and for Valentine's Day one year, it was another fancy eatery. She was curious as to how a college student could afford such places, especially a scholarship student. Then she found out that Nigel was an heir to the Pierre International fortune. Priscilla had heard of the company; her mother used to use their curry powder and chili sauce all the time. Priscilla saw her chance: Nigel was a ticket to a better life than she could afford on her own.

But reality and fantasy were two different things. She and Nigel married right after graduation. Maya came along almost a year later. Priscilla hadn't wanted children so soon, but Nigel had been ecstatic. Little Miles came along a year after that. Nigel didn't want Priscilla to work, so Priscilla joined the scores of nannies in the park every day, so that the children could get some fresh air and exercise. Unfortunately for the children, Priscilla was still searching for that maternal instinct, that overriding motherly love that was supposed to come along with giving birth. They were her kids, and she took care of them but if they were to die tomorrow, Priscilla didn't think that she would grieve that much.

Priscilla got off at the Clinton-Washington station, then walked to a co-op building on Clinton Avenue. She signed in at the guard booth and waited for the guard to phone up and announce her presence. After getting buzzed into the building, she rode the elevator to the third floor and knocked on the door of apartment 3A. Trey Jacobson answered the door with a scowl.

"You couldn't wait until a decent hour to come by?" Trey grumbled as Priscilla pushed past him and removed her scarf.

"I can't stay long. Nigel and the kids were taking a nap when I left." She draped the scarf over the back of the couch and sat down. Her purse was transferred from her shoulder to her lap.

Trey sat down in the custom-made breakfast nook and watched Priscilla. He noted the stress lines around her eyes and the disheveled state of her hair. It had been pulled back into a haphazard ponytail, which displayed dulled ends that badly needed trimming and conditioning. Her clothes seemed to be a size too big, and tension was evident in the hands that gripped her large leather purse. He shook his head in disgust. Despite all that, she was still fine to him. "So, what do you want?"

"You didn't tell me he was going to go to jail!" Tears welled up in Priscilla's eyes as she remembered the sound of Nigel's voice when he called her from there.

"You told me you wanted him out of the way, and that you wanted more money." Trey shrugged. "I just killed two birds with one stone."

"But that package...I didn't know that it was drugs!"

Trey rose and got a beer from his refrigerator. He didn't offer Priscilla anything. "What the hell did you think it was? I damn sure wasn't giving him a birthday present. And it was no different than the packages that you deliver in Brooklyn." He sat back in the chair and cocked his head at Priscilla. "Don't tell me you're feeling guilty?"

Priscilla kneaded the sides of the purse. "I mean...he sounded so sad. And he's exhausted, and worried that he'll lose his job. Nigel can't handle prison, Trey. I didn't mean for it to get this far."

Trey almost choked on his beer. "You didn't mean for it to get this far?" His tone was incredulous. "Don't even try to play me like that, Priscilla. Not when you were the one up in my grill at the Quasar Charity Golf Tournament earlier this year. Talking about how you hate your life; how you wish you had more money to do the things you wanted; how your husband wasn't as successful as some of his cousins." Trey took another

114

sip of beer and eyed Priscilla over the bottle. "That was you, wasn't it?"

Priscilla looked around the living room that belonged to the man with whom she had become involved, for better or for worse. It was filled with the latest in high-tech gadgetry: 50" flat-screen HDTV; DVD player; Xbox; Bang & Olufsen home theatre system. A large painting of a voluptuous, nude woman hung on one wall, below which stood a medium-sized shelf filled with CDs and DVDs. His furniture was butter-soft dark brown leather that rested upon a cream and brown patterned area rug. Beneath the rug was beige shag carpet. The kitchen alcove boasted stainless steel Viking appliances and stripped pine cabinets, The dining room table, also pine, had slipcovered chairs. Everything looked as if it was fresh off the showroom floor; Trey didn't seem to spend much time at home. Priscilla thought of the used appliances and constant clutter of toys that filled their apartment on the floor of the apartment she shared with Nigel. She turned to see that Trey's eyes were still upon her.

"I didn't mean for it to get this far," Priscilla repeated quietly. "I just wanted Nigel to go away for a while, give me some space while I figured out what I wanted to do."

"He is going away for a while. A long while." Trey looked at Priscilla with thinly veiled contempt. When you made a choice, you should stand by it, no matter what. Priscilla was like so many others he'd known: bold at first, but then freaking out at the first sign of trouble. She wasn't the first person in the world to sell her soul, then grow weary of the price. Too bad she was married; she and Jeff would have been perfect for each other. But maybe not; she would have killed Jeff in bed. "Anyway, I have some more deliveries for you to make. But before you do…come here. I got something for you."

Priscilla clutched her purse again. Her eyes widened.

"Girl, I'm not going to take your purse," Trey said with irritation. "Come here."

Priscilla set the purse aside and stood on wobbly knees before walking over to Trey. They stared at each other before he removed a glassine bag of iridescent white powder and a small mirror from the sugar bowl on the table. Priscilla wiped her nose as her greedy eyes watched Trey expertly chop up the Blizzard, before arranging it in six precise lines. He reached into the bowl again and removed a hollow gold tube, and pushed both toward Priscilla. She bent her head and quickly inhaled the white powder.

Priscilla wiped her nose again when she was done and leaned back. The Blizzard did its job; first the power surged through her brain like a rogue snowstorm, strong and electric. She blinked as colors became brighter, textures more defined. Then the morphine derivatives in the mixture descended upon her hyped nerve endings as the snowstorm turned to a gentle snowfall. The methylphenidate controlled the undercurrent of hyperactivity beneath the snowfall; an animal burrowing to avoid the storm, waiting for it to end. Priscilla felt in control, smart, sexy. She looked at Trey with drug-fogged eyes and licked her lips.

"You know what to do." Trey watched with a cruel pleasure as she walked over on her knees and undid the fly on his pants. Pleasure raced up Trey's spine as Priscilla took him into her mouth with the enthusiasm

of an upper echelon porn star. The overhead track
lights played rhythmically upon her wedding rings.

EIGHT

The next day, Sebastian, Alex, Jonathan, and Trackie watched a soccer match on television. The Scott home was relatively quiet; Tia and the rest of the female cousins had gone shopping and sightseeing. Janelle and Michelle were with their parents and other siblings at Michelle's house in the Canarsie section of Brooklyn. Stephen was at the Home Depot, his home away from home. Other relatives were out and about, visiting and just enjoying being in New York.

The doorbell rang, but no one budged. "Get the door, Trackie," Dante ordered the younger man.

"Why do I have to get the door?" Trackie whined, his gray eyes glued to the screen. "You're nearest to it."

Jonathan slapped Trackie on the back of his head. "Get off your arse and get the bloody door."

"Ow!" Trackie grumbled and rubbed the back of his head, but did as he was told. Moments later he returned, with Nigel in tow. Nigel shifted from foot to foot, his hands shoved in the pockets of blue jeans that sagged a bit on his thin frame. The tails of his white shirt weren't tucked in and peeked from beneath his fleece-lined leather jacket.

"What's up, Nigel?" Alex called out. The others murmured similar greetings as everyone paid attention to the match. After a few minutes, Alex noted that Nigel was still in the same spot. "Why you still standing?"

Nigel quickly sat down in the nearest chair, a bedraggled floral-patterned armchair that had seen better days but that Janelle kept for sentimental value. He feigned interest in the game on TV, but he really wanted to talk to Sebastian. During halftime, the men assembled in the kitchen to look for something to eat. As everyone filed back into the living room with plates of sandwiches and potato chips, Nigel saw his chance when Sebastian re-entered the kitchen.

Nigel cleared his throat nervously. "Uh, Sebastian?"

Sebastian removed a handful of napkins from the kitchen table. "Huh?"

"Uh, can I talk to you for a minute?"

Sebastian looked back toward the living room, then back at Nigel. "Now?"

Nigel swallowed. "Yes. Please."

Sebastian stared at Nigel, then shrugged. He sat down at the table and began to eat his sandwich. "Talk," he mumbled around a mouth full of food.

Nigel pulled out a chair and sat opposite Sebastian. "I, uh, just wanted to apologize for yesterday. I was out of line, and I'm sorry."

Sebastian stopped in mid-chew, shocked. Nigel never apologized for anything. Pointing fingers and deflecting blame was more his style, and had been so since they were children. Nothing like an arrest to make a person humble. Sebastian swallowed and said, "Apology accepted. And I apologize for making those comments about you in the pen."

Nigel nodded, his eyes trained on the matching salt and pepper shakers. "But you were right, Sebastian." He played with the salt shaker and blurted out, "I'm scared."

Sebastian found it hard to stay mad at Nigel when he looked so pitiful. "I know, Nigel."

"I didn't do it, Sebastian. I swear, I didn't do anything with those drugs. I didn't even know they were there." Nigel's face took on the pinched expression that had been present in the courtroom.

Sebastian looked at his cousin more closely. The events of the past thirty-six hours had clearly taken their toll on Nigel. There were deep shadows under his eyes and while Nigel had always been slim, it was obvious that he hadn't been eating properly. His skin was dull and he could use a haircut. The jacket and blue jeans looked to be two sizes too big for him.

Nigel took a deep breath. "I need your help, Sebastian." The words came out in a rush. "Look, I know you don't like me. But just this once, could you put that aside and try to keep me from going to jail?" Nigel's breathing quickened. "I can't go to prison, Sebastian. I can't. I'd die in there. And if they try to send me, I'll kill myself before I go."

Sebastian frowned, and remembered Alex's earlier comments about Nigel being a suicide risk. "Nigel, stop with that kind of talk. You have two kids and a wife."

"I'd do it! I'd kill myself." His breaths turned erratic as Nigel began to hyperventilate.

Sebastian rose and yanked open a bottom cabinet, where his mom usually kept her brown paper grocery bags. He retrieved a smaller one and went over to Nigel, who was struggling to get air into his lungs.

Sebastian placed the paper bag over Nigel's mouth and said, "Calm down, Nigel. Just calm down. Take deep breaths." Sebastian watched as Nigel concentrated on the instructions and tried to breathe evenly.

"Hey, Sebastian, you're missing the..." Trackie's voice trailed as he took in the scene before him. "What's the matter with Nigel? Is he sick?"

"Stop talking about him as if he's not here," Sebastian scolded. "He'll be fine."

"But now you're talking about him like he's not here," Trackie pointed out.

Sebastian shot Trackie an annoyed look. "Did you want something, Trackie?"

Trackie's eyes were glued to the expanding and collapsing paper bag that Nigel held to his mouth. "I was just coming to tell you that the second half's started. Brazil's ball."

"Thanks." Sebastian turned his attention back to Nigel, who's breathing had regulated.
"Better?"

Nigel nodded. "Yeah," he said in a weakened voice. "Thanks."

Sebastian noticed that Trackie was still standing in the kitchen, observing his cousins. "Trackie, make yourself useful. Get Nigel some water."

Trackie retrieved a glass from an overhead cabinet and filled it with ice and water. He handed the glass to Nigel, who murmured his thanks and proceeded to drain the glass. Trackie got him a refill. Nigel sipped this time, his eyes unfocused.

Sebastian leaned against the counter and studied Nigel. "Nigel, if you want me to help you, then you'll have to do what I tell you to do. When I ask you questions, I'm not trying to vex you or make you look stupid. I'm asking because the answers will give me the clues necessary to help you get out of this jam. I do this every day; you don't."

Nigel nodded again. "I know, Sebastian. And I appreciate it. Really."

Sebastian didn't quite believe his appreciation; he figured it was the situation talking. "Well, the first thing we need to do is figure out why you were framed. Once we do that, we can figure out who. Now, did the DEA search your house?"

Nigel's face pinched again. He remembered the chaos that had met him and Priscilla when they had returned home. His mother and father had taken the kids back to Uncle Morris's house while he and Priscilla cleaned up. "Yes," he nodded as he swallowed down embarrassment. "They went through everything."

"Okay. When you cleaned up, did you notice that anything was missing? Any papers, furniture, anything?"

Nigel thought about it, then shook his head. "I couldn't really tell. Everything was such a mess. But as far as I could tell, mostly everything was there."

Sebastian snagged some potato chips from his plate and crunched thoughtfully. "Do you keep business stuff at home? Projects you're working on, stuff like that?"

"Sometimes. If it's a big project and I don't want to stay at the office all night, I bring stuff home. I can log into the Quasar database from my laptop, which was issued by the company."

Sebastian was thinking of options. It would be great to access Nigel's files and look through the papers at his home. But he was quite sure that Nigel's house was under surveillance; anyone going in and out would be tagged, and Sebastian couldn't afford that right now. If he was to help Nigel, he'd have to do it through the back door, so to speak, since he wasn't officially assigned to the case. "Where is your laptop?"

"At work. I took to the IT department to get some software upgrades."

Sebastian bit back a sigh. No help there. "What were you working on at your job?"

"The usual stuff," Nigel said. "Some new clients that wanted some swaps done. Doing research on existing deals." He frowned as he remembered what he'd discovered.

Sebastian caught it. "What? What's wrong?"

123

Nigel hesitated. "Well, while I was working late a few nights ago, I overheard two of the junior partners talking about two loan-swapping deals that I had initially worked on. Then, I did some digging and found what seemed to be major discrepancies in the interest rates on the loan swaps." He took another sip of water. "I was trying to figure out how to broach the subject, and to whom, and decided to write it up so that I could get all of the facts down in a logical manner."

"Did you write this report on your computer at work?"

"Yes," Nigel nodded. "I saved it to my personal folder. "

"Is your personal folder on the company computer network?"

"Yeah, but no one else has access to it but me."

Sebastian shook his head. Nigel was so naïve sometimes.

"I can get into his computer files."

Sebastian turned to look at Trackie. He'd forgotten the younger man was there. "What?"

"I said, I can get into his files. Come on, Nigel." Trackie loped out of the room, charged with excitement. Nigel looked at Sebastian, then followed his younger cousin. Sebastian blinked, then brought up the rear. Jonathan, Dante, and Alex noticed the processional and looked at each other, then rose to join the party.

Trackie went downstairs to the bottom level, where Janelle kept her office. As a semi-retired psychologist, she still saw patients occasionally and Trackie, when he was still working on a master's degree in social work at New York University, would visit her sometimes. He still stopped by sometimes to see his aunt, even though he transferred to the John Jay College of Criminal Justice to study criminology. "What's going on?" Jonathan asked.

"I'm going to hack into Nigel's company server, so we can see the research he did on some shady projects." He sat down behind her desktop computer and booted it up.

"Hold up." Alex held up both hands in a "stop" gesture. "Did I hear you correctly? Did you say that you were going to hack into a corporate database? Of Nigel's job?"

"Yep." His fingers flew across the keyboard.

Alex stared at Trackie in disbelief. "Hacking is illegal."

"Only if you get caught."

Alex waved a hand in the air. "Hello, Officer of the Court here."

"And a federal law enforcement officer," Sebastian added.

Trackie looked at the screen and nodded. "Okay, Nigel, what is the URL of your corporate website?"

Sebastian frowned. "Wait; how'd you even get to the Internet? You know my mother's password?"

"She has it taped to the inside of her desk drawer."

Alex shot first Sebastian, then Trackie, an incredulous look. "Okay, I can't be here. Plausible deniability, and all that." He looked at Sebastian. "You, either."

Nigel and Trackie were now huddled in front of the computer. "Come back in ten minutes," Trackie suggested.

Alex saw Sebastian open his mouth to protest. "Let's go, Frat." He grabbed Sebastian's arm and pushed him out of the room.

"But..."

"Let's go." Alex closed the office door firmly behind him.

Fifteen minutes later, they returned to find Nigel and Jonathan poring over sheaves of paper. Trackie was still in front of the computer.

Alex pointed at the papers in Nigel's hands. "What is that?"

"It's my report."

"No." Alex shook his head emphatically. "No, you don't understand how this works. There's this little part of a legal case called discovery; that means that any existing documents, or other physical items regarding your case, are potentially evidence. Evidence that can either set you free, or lock the door of your prison cell. And I am legally obligated to turn these documents over to the prosecution, and vice versa. Now, while we attorneys tend to play a bit fast and loose with discovery rules at one time or the other, the fact remains that the evidence will be turned over, one way or another. That," he stabbed a finger at the papers again, "is evidence and I'd prefer not to know that it exists, because then I'd have to tell opposing counsel or risk disbarment."

"Oh." Nigel swallowed. "Sorry."

"Well, let's walk you through what we've learned so far, and then we'll burn the papers," Jonathan said.

"Now you want to destroy evidence." Alex put his palms over his eyes and took a deep breaths. "Woo saa. Woooooo saaaaaa," he intoned with each breath.

Sebastian didn't know what to think, or do. If this were any other case, he probably wouldn't be having these issues. But he wasn't in San Francisco, with his field office cohorts around him, his Confidential Informants, and his SFPD cronies such as Zachary Demps. Sebastian ran a hand over his close-cropped hair. On one hand, he knew they were in illegal territory. On the other hand, his hands were tied with regard to getting more detailed information on Nigel's situation. Sometimes, a little creativity was in order, especially when dealing with family.

"Calm down." Jonathan's eyes were still trained on the papers. "Nigel said that he was working on two projects that involved a derivative loan swap, but he found that the interest rates on the swap were too high."

Sebastian held up a hand. "I don't speak finance. Break this down to me like I'm a two year-old."

127

"You didn't cover loan swaps when you sat for your MBA?"

"I have a vague recollection of a few paragraphs in a textbook, years ago, but that wasn't my particular area of concentration."

"Right. Well, most companies don't own their properties outright. That could be corporate headquarters, or any buildings within the corporation's portfolio. Regardless of the type of property, odds are that the corporation has taken out a loan on each property, and is paying a mortgage." Jonathan stretched and clasped his hands behind his head. This was his area of expertise. "Companies need what are called derivative loan swaps in order to gain more favorable loan numbers. A derivative loan is when a lender or borrower transfers risk of loan default to a third party, while keeping the loan or their books for tax purposes. A swap is when two entities agree upon such a loan transfer.

"There are two main types of loans: a fixed-rate loan, where the interest rate on the loan stays the same throughout the life of the loan. And an adjustable rate mortgage, or ARM, where the interest rates fluctuate over the life of the loan, usually based on the London Inter-Bank Offering Rate, or LIBOR. When there is a derivative loan swap, two companies basically enter into an agreement for each to take on the other's loan rates for a specific period of time."

"And they would do that...why?" Sebastian asked.

"To free up cash flow."

"Okay, so how does this swap thing work?"

Jonathan leaned forward for emphasis. "Let's say that Company A has a fixed loan rate at 5.6%, and Company B has a variable, or ARM rate, at 5.0%. Company B wants to do some restructuring and it may be more beneficial for them to have a fixed rate instead of a variable one, due to the finances involved in such. It sits down with Company A and proposes a swap, whereby Company A would pay the variable rate for Company B and Company B would pay the fixed rate for Company A, for the remaining period of the loan. Everybody's happy, provided that the payments are made on time. Better yet, if either company is not pleased with the other's performance, it could back out of the deal with thirty days' notice of doing so. Best of all, such a practice is perfectly legal." Jonathan grinned. "It's quite brilliant, actually."

Everyone except Nigel looked at Jonathan with a blank expression.

"Ohhhhhkay." Alex rubbed his forehead. "What does this have to do with Nigel's discovery?"

"I discovered, through my research, that the interest rates on the saps of two companies in particular, Cauldrice Properties and Landries Real Estate Holdings, were way above the norm" Nigel said. "In a normal loan swap, the rate is LIBOR plus 7.5%. But for these projects, it's LIBOR plus 11.5%, plus what seems to be a transactional fee, for a total of 15%. That's unheard of."

Jonathan had gone back to the papers, and paused as he read something else. "Trackie, are you still in the company network?" At the younger man's nod, Jonathan instructed, "Do a search for NTJ Holdings,

129

please." He continued to flip through the papers, pausing every few seconds to read something. "This is odd," he murmured. "Some of these companies have entered swaps, only to terminate their contracts six months later."

"I take it that's not normal?" Dante asked.

"Not at all." Jonathan continued to read the columns of dates and figures. "When you enter a swap, it's usually for a period of about five years, depending upon the reason behind the swap."

"What do you mean?"

"Say that you own a company and you need to restructure the organization," Jonathan explained. "You purchased the building that houses your company with an adjustable rate mortgage loan, or ARM, that is currently at 4.6 percent due to the Federal Reserve shaving another percentage off the interest rate."

Alex smiled. He loved it when the interest rate dropped because stocks and bonds usually went up, which was good news for his portfolio.

"Anyway," Jonathan continued, "a company across town has a fixed mortgage rate of 5.2% on the loan for their building."

"This is definitely a hypothetical situation," Dante mumbled. He thought of the interest rate on the loan when he first purchased his office building in downtown San Pablo, which he now owned free and clear. Real estate prices in the Bay Area were atrocious. Add not-so-favorable interest rates on top of that, and one was tempted to rent for the rest of one's life. Or move out of California.

"So you think that 'Hey, if I could get a fixed mortgage rate for the next five years, while we restructure, that would be great. We won't have to worry about whether the interest rate will rise and deplete the funds needed for the restructuring.' Do you follow me?"

Sebastian and the others nodded.

"So you contact a third party, usually a firm specializing in derivative loan swaps and the like, such as Quasar, and you ask them to orchestrate the deal. Once the deal goes through, you agree to pay the other company 7.5%, which includes the LIBOR. Your company would pay 5.2% on a specified day of each month. The other company, on that same day, would pay the difference between their fixed rate of 5.2% and the variable rate. Is everyone still with me?"

"For the most part," Sebastian answered. The others nodded in agreement.

"Now, the other company would pay you more if the rate drops, and less if the rate rises. This would continue for the period of the loan, which is normally five years, or until they cancel prior to the payment date, whichever comes first. And if there is to be a cancellation of terms, then a thirty-day written notice prior to the next payment date would be required." Jonathan finished his explanation and looked at his cousins. "Any questions?"

"Yeah." Alex leaned against the doorjamb and crossed his arms. "So, companies would agree to a swap for a period of five years?"

"That's correct," Jonathan said. "Five years is the standard. A lot of work goes into these swaps, and banks value stability above all else. They want to make sure that they know when their money is coming."

"But a company can back out with thirty days' notice?" Dante asked. "That's what you just said."

Jonathan nodded. "Yes. It's not unheard of, but when entering into a swap one usually knows whom one is dealing with. To suddenly pull the plug would reek of something underhanded, unless there was good reason, such as one of the companies filing bankruptcy or nonsense of that sort." He waved the sheaf of papers in his hand. "That's what just caught my attention. For the past year, there have been quite a few swap deals ending after six months to the day."

"What?" Nigel held out his hands for the papers. Jonathan handed them over. Nigel flipped through them. "You're right, Jon. I didn't even see that. What does this mean?"

"It means that someone in your firm is shady, and is probably getting kickbacks from those deals," Alex said. "We need to find out who is doing those deals. That may help us find who framed you."

"Kickbacks?" Sebastian thought for a moment. He looked at Nigel and Jonathan. "How much are we talking about?"

Jonathan shrugged. "Depends on the size of the deal. But if these deals are going through at the inflated rate of 15%, then we're talking hundreds of thousands of dollars, maybe even millions."

"You add up enough of those deals, and you can scrape up a nice chunk of change," Dante mused. "Enough to, say, finance major drug buys."

Sebastian looked at him sharply. "You think?" Sarcasm was heavy in his voice.

"That's what I would do, if I were in that situation and of a criminal mind." Dante grinned.

Sebastian rolled his eyes. "Pots and kettles. Anyway, so now we not only have to find out who is doing these deals, but what they're doing with the kickbacks."

"NTJ Holdings is listed as the principals in those deals," Jonathan added. "Trackie, did you find anything?"

"NTJ Holdings." Nigel swallowed. "Nathaniel Trey Jacobson."

"Who?" Sebastian asked.

"His full name is Nathaniel Jacobson the Third, but everyone calls him Trey. He's the son of the company's founder and CEO, Nathaniel Jacobson, Jr."

"The owner's son?" Alex's grin was best described as wolfish. "This gets better and better. Reasonable doubt, here we come!"

"I'm not finding any NTJ Holdings in the client database," Trackie announced.

"Well, they've been rather busy for a company that is not included in the Quasar client database."

Sebastian looked at Nigel. "When someone brokers a deal, who's in on it? Who are the key people involved?"

"Well, Nathaniel Jacobson is the founder and CEO. He handles all of the really big deals," Nigel started. "But he's been mainly focusing on new clients. He's planning to take Quasar public next year, and is stoking people to purchase initial public stock offerings in the company." He scratched the nape of his neck, thinking. "Most of the day-to-day stuff falls to Malcolm Jennings. He's a senior partner and pretty much the second-in-command, like a Chief Operating Officer, though not on paper. Curtis Harris is the other senior partner. Then there are two junior partners, Jeffrey Nixon and Trey Jacobson."

"NTJ Holdings." Alex shook his head. "Could he be any more obvious?"

"It fits," Jonathan conceded. "And this Trey Jacobson would be high enough on the inside to pull off something like this."

"Trey wouldn't do anything like that," Nigel argued. "Why should he? That's his father's company. He has a good position, he's an only child, and stands to inherit the company one day. Why jeopardize all that?"

"I wonder what the relationship is like between Trey and his father," Trackie mused. At Nigel's confused look he said, "It's the psychologist in me. Do they get along, Nigel, as far as you can tell?"

Nigel shrugged. "I guess. I don't see them interact much. Nate travels a lot, so he's not in the office most of the time."

"I would like to know how Trey feels about this IPO business," Jonathan said. "If this is indeed his eventual inheritance, then he might not be too pleased at it going public. Once it does so, anyone with a majority holding of stock would control the company."

"Nate wouldn't let that happen," Nigel protested. "He'd keep the majority stake in the company."

"For now," Dante chimed in. "But in business, it's survival of the fittest and Quasar is a small firm. If any of the stockholders decided to pool their resources, it's quite possible that Nate could lose control of the firm. Happens all the time."

"You're all on the wrong track." Nigel's face had taken on a stubborn look familiar to his cousins, and they knew that he would not be swayed.

"Log off, Trackie," Jonathan said in a weary tone. Trackie complied and shut the computer down. Silence descended upon the room.

"I hope you're right, Nigel," Alex said. "'Cause if you're not, you may not have a job to go back to."

NINE

"I've been thinking," Jonathan mused as he, Sebastian, and Alex walked back from a run to a local bodega. "It would be nice to speak to this Malcolm bloke."

"Why?" Alex asked.

"Well, according to Nigel, he's more like the second-in-command at Quasar. That means that not much should get past him. It could be that he knows a lot more than Nigel knows, like who could have pulled off this swap fraud."

"Unless he's the one who perpetrated the fraud," Alex argued. "It's not like he would admit it."

"But we don't know that, do we? If we got into Quasar to speak with him, he may give something away. " He looked at Sebastian. "Isn't' that what you law enforcement types do? Read people's body language?"

"Wait a minute," Sebastian protested. "I know you don't think that I'm going to talk to him."

"How else will we get to the bottom of what's going on with Nigel?"

Sebastian was exasperated. "How many times do I have to say this? While I am a federal agent, I work in San Francisco, plus I'm related to Nigel. I cannot formally investigate this case. If I walked into Quasar and flashed my badge, I have no doubt it would get back to the Special Agents who really are investigating, and that would not be a good look."

"Who said you had to flash your badge?"

"Then how else, and why else, would I be there? I don't work in finance. Corporate types like this Malcolm don't usually accept walk-in appointments. Their calendars are probably books weeks, if not months, in advance."

"Jonathan could do it," Alex chimed in.

Jonathan whipped around to stare at Alex. "I beg your pardon?"

"You're the one talking about 'we' can do this or that."

"I meant the general 'we'," Jonathan protested, "as in, Team Nigel. Not 'we', as in, 'me'."

"You have the financial credentials that would probably interest someone like Malcolm. And, you work for an international bank. Wouldn't that be a point in your favor, since a small firm like Quasar would probably be looking to expand its clientele?"

Jonathan dismissed his statement. "I couldn't possibly do that."

"You were real quick to dangle me as bait a few minutes ago," Sebastian pointed out. "And you're better qualified; a meeting with Malcolm would look normal for you."

"But like you said, executives normally don't accept unscheduled appointments." He used the British pronunciation, *un-SHED-yuled*. "And, I work in a separate area of finance. Malcolm would, or should, know that, once I gave my name. I can't just make an appointment for some specious reason."

"Oh, so you roll like that, J?" Alex grinned.

Jonathan returned the grin. "I do have a certain reputation within the banking world, Alex. It's done me well, so far."

Alex shrugged. "Just say that you're in town on a quick business trip and you don't have much time. And if Quasar is looking to do an IPO next year, then you could use that angle. Say that you are feeling them out to do a private investment, or something."
"I don't know..."

"Come on." Alex clapped him on the back. "We're doing this for Team Nigel, remember?"

"Well..." Jonathan weighed his options. "I'll see what I can do, but Sebastian comes with me."

Sebastian started to protest, then stopped at Jonathan's glare. "Alright," he conceded. "I'll come too."

~ ~ ~

Jonathan and Sebastian approached the reception desk at Quasar. Jonathan never traveled, even for pleasure, without at least two of his bespoke suits. Today he chose a dark gray lightweight flannel suit with a faint chalk pinstripe that brought out his eyes, paired with a pale blue shirt and silver and blue-patterned tie, with a matching pocket square. Sapphire and silver cufflinks winked at his wrists, and his square-toed black leather shoes gleamed. Since he and Sebastian were of similar height and build, and since Sebastian had nothing dressier than khaki pants, Jonathan lent him his other suit: a black wool worsted, with an aqua and black mini-hound's-tooth patterned tie, and a white dress shirt with regular cuffs. A handkerchief in the same fabric as the tie peeked from the breast pocket.

The attractive receptionist held up one index finger as she spoke into her headset. Her brass nameplate read, "Assata Johnson."

"Yes….that's correct…yes…we'll do that. Thank you again for calling Quasar. Have a good day. Bye now." She disconnected the call and turned her attention to the men in front of her. "Welcome to Quasar. How may I help you?"

"Good day." Jonathan switched his briefcase to his opposite hand as he reached into his inner pocket for his black eel skin business card holder. "Jonathan Heath, to see Malcolm Jennings." He removed a card and offered it to Assata.

"Of course." Assata took the card and looked at Sebastian expectantly. When he remained silent, she raised an eyebrow. "One moment please." She pressed a button with a manicured finger and murmured into the headset before disconnecting the call. "Someone will be right with you, gentlemen. Please, have a seat." She gestured to the plump sofa and chairs in the reception area before turning her attention back to her computer. Sebastian let his eyes rove around the tastefully appointed lobby, and caught Assata's curious gaze before she hastily lowered her eyes.

The soft thud of high heels on the thick carpet caught the attention of the two men. A striking, petite woman in a tailored black suit and ivory silk blouse strode toward them. Her cream-colored pearl necklace and teardrop earrings had a muted glow underneath the fluorescent lights. "Good morning, gentlemen," she stated with crisp diction. "I'm Alicia Fisher. Mr. Jennings will see you now." She turned and strutted back down the hall on three-inch stiletto heels, the two men in tow. She stopped before the open door of a large corner office that overlooked the busy streets below and offered a decent view of the New York skyline. A man with close-cropped hair sat behind a mahogany and glass desk, looking down at a handful of papers. A large silver frame to his right held an 8" x 10" color photo of a pretty woman with deep dimples and a wide smile.

Alicia gestured the men into the office. Malcolm stood and came around the desk with a charming bonhomie. "Malcolm Jennings," he said as he held an outstretched hand to Jonathan.

"Jonathan Heath. Thank you for seeing me on such short notice."

"It's not every day that a man of your reputation and organization stops by Quasar." He looked over at Sebastian and held out his hand again. "Malcolm Jennings."

"Sebastian Scott." He tried not to scoff aloud at Malcolm's bone-crusher grip, calculated to intimidate.

Malcolm shook his hand and gestured at the two chairs in front of his desk. "Please, sit down. Can I get you two anything? Water? Coffee?"

"I'm fine, thank you." Sebastian declined as well.

"That will be all, Alicia. Thanks." Malcolm went back to his chair and leaned forward. "Mr. Heath, you stated that Barclays was seeking another U.S. partner?"

Jonathan tried not to squirm at this fib. "Yes. We are always in the market for partnerships that will further enhance our global brand. I've heard interesting things about Quasar and your work with derivative loan swaps. While I was in town, I thought it'd be worth my while to take a meeting and see if there was mutual benefit."

"I see. Well, tell me exactly what you're looking to accomplish, and we can talk about it." He kept glancing at Sebastian, who had yet to contribute to the conversation.

"We may be interested in some swaps with a few properties we hold in both New York. Perhaps Quasar could provide services in that area."

"Really?" Malcolm steepled his hands. "That's interesting. I would think that with a significant presence in the United States, especially here in New York, that you wouldn't need a third party to handle swaps for you."

"We get a lot of business. It never hurts to outsource when needed."

"I agree. However, Mr. Heath, you normally deal with global finance and risk management, specifically in the Asia Pacific regions. Loan swaps aren't exactly your wheelhouse, are they?"

Jonathan shrugged. "Diversification is always important. Speaking of which, I'm more inclined to discuss an investment of a more personal nature." At Malcolm's inquisitive expression, he continued. "Rumor has it that Quasar will be making an initial public offering next year."

Malcolm tilted his head in a noncommittal fashion.

"If those rumors are true, I may be interested in purchasing some shares with my personal funds. To that end, I thought it best to get a look at the operation in person, since I was already here in the States."

"Right." Malcolm looked over at Sebastian. "Mr. Scott, in what capacity do you work for Barclays?"

"I don't."

"Then with what financial institution are you affiliated?"

"I'm not."

Malcolm frowned. "Then what do you do?" He tapped his steepled fingers against his chin as he stared at Sebastian. "Are you even in finance?"

"No."

"Then why..." Malcolm's voice trailed off while he looked back at Jonathan, then back to Sebastian. "Are you two related?"

Jonathan blinked. "Why?"

"Because you both have the same eyes. In fact, there's a guy who works here--or, at least he does on paper-- who has eyes that look like yours."

"Oh?"

"Yes, 'oh'." Malcolm mimicked Jonathan's British accent. He waited for them to answer amid the growing tension, then sat back in his chair. "Mr. Heath, I think we can agree that you, on behalf of Barclays, have no interest in Quasar as a client or partner. I'm more inclined to believe that you want to purchase shares of Quasar when we go public, but you haven't sold me on that, either."

"Perhaps," Jonathan conceded. "But things can change. I golf with the group chief executive of Barclays once a month; a well-placed word could prove beneficial, especially given your eventual IPO next year. And I always look to diversify my personal portfolio."

"Indeed." He steepled his fingers again and eyed Jonathan over them. "Why are you really here?"

Jonathan looked at Sebastian. Sebastian answered, "We wanted to speak with you about one of your employees: Nigel Pierre."

"Ah." Malcolm leaned back in his chair. "You're here about Nigel. I'm afraid you may be wasting your time. I don't have much to say about him." He turned toward Sebastian. "You never said who you work for."

"You didn't ask."

"Touché." Malcolm nodded to concede the point. "So who is your employer? It's certainly not a bank."

"The Drug Enforcement Administration."

"A Fed." Malcolm stared at Sebastian. "Wait a minute. Nigel mentioned once that he had a cousin who was a DEA Agent in California. San Francisco, I think."

Sebastian inclined his head in agreement. "That would be me."

"Interesting. Well, I think it's safe to say that this is a little outside of your jurisdiction, even for a federal officer. Not to mention, a conflict of interest. In fact," he gave a snide grin, "do the DEA agents here in New York know that you are here right now?"

"I'm not officially investigating Nigel's case."

"You're not *officially* investigating." Malcolm's grin widened. "So, you wouldn't mind if I called the Special Agents handling this case, and told them you dropped by for a chat?"

That was the last thing that Sebastian wanted. "You could. I wouldn't recommend it."

Sebastian and Malcolm engaged in a staring contest. Suddenly, Malcolm let out a bark of laughter. "I like you, Special Agent Scott. You've got balls." He turned to Jonathan. "And you, Mr. Heath? What is your interest in this case?"

"Nigel is my cousin as well."

"Well, well. A family affair." Malcolm shifted to a more comfortable position, a lion at home in his jungle. "I probably shouldn't speak with you without our corporate attorney present."

Sebastian laced his fingers across his midsection. "Then call him."

"Her," Malcolm corrected, "and Ruth's off the premises at the moment." He paused, then shrugged. "I think I can answer your questions without getting myself, or Quasar, in legal trouble. Since neither of you are here in an official capacity, anything I say can't be used against me." He settled himself more comfortably in his chair. "Alright. Ask away. You have ten minutes."

"Thank you." Sebastian leaned forward. "Nigel mentioned that you've worked closely with him on some projects in Miami."

"One project in Miami, and yes, I did."

"He told us that you are the firm's expert on derivatives. Is that true?"

Malcolm's dark brown eyes were calculating even as he schooled his facial features into a neutral expression. "I suppose." He picked up a black Montblanc Meisterstück pen and twirled it in his long fingers. "I do have input on most of the derivative transactions that transpire in this firm."

"Then perhaps you can explain to us how derivative loan swaps work."

Malcolm looked at Jonathan. "Do I really need to explain this to you, Mr. Heath?"

"No, I'm well aware of how they work," Jonathan smiled. "But I am curious as to why a firm would be charging a 15% interest rate on a swap, including LIBOR."

Malcolm raised his eyebrows. "I know of no company in their right mind that would enter into a deal with a 15% interest rate on the swap. That's way too high, and you know it."

"I agree. The rate is way too high for a swap. So no one in your firm would even offer a deal like that?"

"Of course not," Malcolm snapped. "We may not be the largest or most well-known banking firm, but we don't hire idiots, either. And no one here would broker a transaction with those preposterous rates, or they won't work here very long."

"Have you ever heard of NTJ Holdings?" Sebastian asked.

"NTJ?" Malcolm paused to think. "No," he shook his head, "can't say that I have. Are they an investment banking firm?"

"Has Quasar ever done any business with NTJ?"

Malcolm's eyes darkened in confusion. "What's this all about? Who is NTJ? Do I need to call Ruth after all?"

"So you've never heard of NTJ?"

"I just told you I didn't."

"Mr. Jennings," Sebastian asked yet again, "you have no knowledge of any clients with the name of NTJ Holdings? Or of any subsidiaries of Quasar Financial Services?"

Malcolm sighed loudly. "How many times do I have to say it? For the last time, no, I do not know of any clients with the name of NTJ Holdings, and there are definitely no Quasar subsidiaries with that name." A large vein throbbed on Malcolm's forehead as his face reddened. "Now tell me what the hell this is all about, or you can speak to me further through my attorney."

"Can you explain how Quasar could do business with a client of which you are not aware?"

"Yes, I'm sure! I'm the de-facto second-in-command here. There's not much that I don't know about, with regard to the day-to-day and pending operations of Quasar." Malcolm stopped and rose from his chair, clearly agitated. He looked out of the large window, which gave him a breathtaking view of the Hudson River and Liberty Island. For a few moments he watched a Circle Line ferry make its way along the river, full of tourists. "There have been no subsidiaries with that name, past or present, under the auspices of Quasar. And there are no plans for one to be created in the future." Malcolm turned and looked at Sebastian and Jonathan. "Did Nigel tell you this?"

"No." Technically, Trackie found the information during his hack, but Malcolm didn't need to know that.

"Right." Malcolm cursed and strode back over to his desk.

Sebastian switched tracks. "What is your assessment of Nigel Pierre?"

"My assessment?" He resumed his seat and smoothed down his hunter green and gold-patterned tie, which complemented his pale yellow dress shirt. "Nigel is a capable young man. We wouldn't have hired him if he weren't."

"Just 'capable'?" Sebastian saw Jonathan frown in his peripheral vision.

"You're reading a whole lot into that one word. Nigel had the necessary education and experience that was required to work at Quasar in his capacity."

"And what capacity was that, exactly?"

Malcolm sat and fiddled with the suspenders that matched his tie. "He was hired as a junior financial analyst."

It was Sebastian's turn to frown. He tried to recall some of Nigel's work experience. He knew that Nigel had done the requisite stint in Pierre International, as most of the grandchildren had who were old enough to work. But surely he had done enough to be more than a junior analyst? He'd have to ask Jonathan about it later.

Malcolm nodded. "Yes. While Nigel had the necessary education and experience for this position, we felt that he could use a bit more investment banking experience. A junior analyst position would give him that experience, while allowing him to grow into the next level."

"How long has he been working for you?"

"Just over two years now."

"What does a junior analyst do? If he still needs more experience, I assume that you didn't give him tasks that he could screw up."

Malcolm steepled his fingers again. "We don't hire people with the assumption that they are going to screw up. Nigel was given duties commensurate with his status within Quasar, and his qualifications."

"And he worked with you, correct? On some deals?"

"That is correct." A slight frown crossed Malcolm's face.

"In Miami?"

"Yes." Malcolm's frown deepened. "We do a lot of work with Miami-Dade County, enough to justify an office branch down there."

"What was your most recent project down there?"

"We worked on a swap between a Cuban art museum and a shopping complex."

"And what happened?"

Malcolm raised an eyebrow. "What do you mean, what happened? The deal is still pending. We're hammering out some minor details in the proposal, but I anticipate that we will secure the contract shortly."

"What was Nigel's role in this deal?" Jonathan asked.

"He was the analyst assigned to the account, under me," Malcolm explained. "He helped draw up the paperwork, prepared a risk analysis, stuff like that."

"Was it possible that Nigel was cooking up a cocaine buy and distribution scheme behind your back."

Malcolm snorted. "Nigel Pierre buying and/or distributing cocaine?" He shook his head and chuckled. "That's funny. Nigel was--is--a straight arrow. And he didn't have the expertise or authority to structure deals or field questions that were beyond a more general nature. Anything involving the intricacies of the project were left to me." He checked his Breitling watch. "I have a meeting in a few minutes, so let's wrap this up."

"So basically, what you're saying was that Nigel was a lower-level employee who was in the wrong place at the wrong time," Sebastian summarized.

"I'm saying that Nigel was a competent employee who seemed happy with his work. It's been my observation that those who seek outside activities are not content with what they have. Now, I don't know much about his home life, other than he is married with two young kids. So maybe you need to check there. But as far as Quasar goes, Nigel is a long shot to stick with a cocaine trafficking rap." Malcolm rose, signaling that the interview was over. He retrieved his suit jacket from the back of his chair. "Now, if you gentlemen would excuse me, I have to meet with a client offsite."

Jonathan and Sebastian rose. "Thank you for your time, Mr. Jennings. He and Malcolm exchanged one last handshake. "I'll be in touch."

On impulse, Sebastian asked, "Would it be possible to get a copy of Nigel's résumé? The one he submitted with his application?"

Malcolm slid his arms into the jacket as he glanced at Sebastian. "Why?"

"It would help us check out his previous employers," Sebastian lied. "Maybe one of them could give us more information as to his personal activities, since Nigel has not been with Quasar that long."

Malcolm picked up a black leather briefcase and nodded. "Fine. If you could wait a few minutes in the lobby, I'll have a copy brought out to you."

"Thank you." After they left, Malcolm looked at his watch and set down his briefcase. He had some digging of his own to do, and had just enough time to get started before his lunch appointment. He picked up the phone and made a call.

Jonathan and Sebastian only had to wait a few minutes before Alicia reappeared ten minutes later. She held a large, sealed white envelope that bore the Quasar logo. She handed it to Jonathan, then turned smartly on her heel and went back to the executive suite. When Jonathan and Sebastian were caught up in the human traffic outside of the building, Sebastian asked, "Well? What did you think?"

"That was an interesting exchange." Jonathan matched his stride to the briskness of everyone else's.

"Yeah, it was. Something's not right."

"I agree."

Sebastian shook his head. "I'm not an investment banker, but it seems that they hired Nigel for reasons other than his expertise, or rather, lack thereof."

Jonathan shrugged as he sidestepped a small mound of smeared dog poop "It's not uncommon to hire for connections. I'd need a closer look at Nigel's résumé before I could make further commentary. But for now, let's find a place to get a nosh. I'm famished after all that verbal sparring and posturing with Malcolm Jennings."

"For real. I'd take a drug cartel over that dog-and-pony show any day."

Over sandwiches and beer, the men discussed Nigel's employment at Quasar. Jonathan removed Nigel's résumé from the envelope and scanned it. "Okay." Jonathan reread the document slowly before shaking his head. "Interesting."

"What?" Sebastian craned his neck to look at the résumé as well, albeit upside down.

Jonathan tossed the paper down. "This is complete bollocks. Nigel shouldn't have been hired for that position. I certainly wouldn't have done so."

"Why?"

Jonathan ticked off his reasons on his fingers. "Nigel doesn't have the requisite education that most people at that level have. His undergraduate degree was in philosophy, and he only took a few business courses at Amherst." He ticked off another point. "Next, Nigel has almost no real work experience. He had internships at two top-ten investment banking firms over two summers during college, and worked at the family company during high school and the summer right after high school graduation, before going back to the family company. Which is another thing; why didn't either of those banking firms offer him a job?

And why did he only get internships for two summers, instead of four? And thirdly," he ticked off yet another point, "he has no postgraduate business degree. An MBA would have been helpful at this point; while his work experience wasn't substantive, he had enough to pull that off." Jonathan popped a French fry into his mouth.

"Then why hire him? What could Quasar possibly gain by hiring Nigel in that capacity?"

"Money and connections. Remember when Nigel said earlier that Quasar was getting ready to do an initial public offering on the company stock?"

"Yeah," Sebastian nodded. "And Malcolm more or less confirmed that. So?"

"So, if you were a small firm looking to expand your business, it would be natural for inquire into overseas opportunities as well. That's why I dangled that bit about golfing with the global client manager, and putting a word in. I checked with some of my colleagues in Britain. Word on the street is that Quasar has been checking into some things in London."

Sebastian stared at Jonathan, waiting for the rest of the explanation. "Okay. You're saying all this to say what?"

Jonathan rolled his eyes heavenward. "You have undergraduate degrees in economics and International

Studies, and an MBA with a concentration in international business, and you still can't figure it out? Don't be daft, Sebastian." He leaned against the dresser and crossed his arms across his chest. "You know that business is about connections, Sebastian. Quid pro quo. The question is hardly ever 'What can I do for you" but rather, 'What can you do for me?' In this case, Nigel is valuable by virtue of what he represents: Pierre International."

"PI?" Sebastian frowned. "Why?"

Jonathan shook his head. "Don't you read the annual reports? Or at least your dividend statements." At Sebastian's shrug, Jonathan sighed. "Anyway, should you deign to pick up one of those reports someday, you'll find that Pierre International made about $224 million last year, and that was just in the duty-free shops in Trinidad and Tobago. If you add in the sales from the outlets in London, New York and Miami, the figures go up to just over $350 million."

Sebastian was stunned. "The company made that much money?"

Jonathan nodded. "Papa has quite the brilliant business mind. Now that was the gross income, but the net figures are still around $275 million. Right now, the company's net worth is over $4 billion."

"So Nigel was hired as an in to the company," Sebastian mused. "Interesting."

"Happens all the time, especially in business. It's not what you know, it's who you know. For Quasar to get business from PI would be a significant coup. And Nigel would be the perfect conduit, by virtue of him working for Quasar and being the grandson of the founder and CEO. Not to mention, his trust fund inheritance in the upcoming years."

Sebastian shook his head. "But PI, successful though it seems, is not a major condiment company like Heinz or Kraft Foods."

"In America, no." Jonathan waved a hand in dismissal. "It's all semantics and perception. Heinz and Kraft have excellent branding strategies and are easily recognizable, and thus considered more popular. That is true. But PI is more like that American cosmetics company...what's it called..." Jonathan snapped his fingers in an effort to jog his memory. "You know, the one that has the big pink cars."

"Mary Kay?" Sebastian was amused.

"Precisely. Though they are not carried in department stores like other, more popular cosmetic lines, Mary Kay is actually the number-one selling cosmetics line in the United States."

"And what do you know about cosmetics?" Sebastian teased.

"Well, I once dated someone who sold it on the side."

Sebastian stared at Jonathan. "You once dated a Mary Kay consultant? You?"

Jonathan shrugged. "This was right after university, shortly before I returned to London. She came by to give me a complimentary facial. The rest, as they say, is history."

The cousins shared a laugh as they dumped their food detritus in the garbage and left the restaurant.

~~~

Sebastian's cell phone rang and he looked down at the display: it was Zachary. "Talk to me," Sebastian answered.

"You owe me so big," Zachary replied.

"That good, huh?"

"When do I ever half-step?"

"Alright," Sebastian laughed. "Whatcha got for me?"

"Well," Zachary drawled, "I reached out and touched my ex, who works in Narcotics over in Brooklyn."

"Your ex is a Narcotics detective? Was that on purpose?"

"Shut up. And being that we didn't part on very friendly terms, I had to go through the tortures of the damned to get any info on Blizzard. She is not what you would call the forgiving sort. So naming your firstborn after me would be a nice start toward compensation."

Sebastian rolled his eyes. "Just tell me what you found out."

"Well, we sweated Entrada's people, and one of them folded. He mentioned that Entrada had family in Miami, which includes two brothers who are also in the drug game: heroin and Ecstasy."

"The family that slangs together, stays together."

156

"Something like that. Anyway, one of the brothers met a friend of a friend who was looking to provide new laundering opportunities, namely through the investment banking industry. Guess how the money was being washed?"

"Loan swaps?"

Zachary snorted. "You don't sound surprised, and you shouldn't be. Anyway, I ran the names by my ex, which got her pretty excited. Seems that one of the preferred laundering businesses belongs to this Dominican guy named Saldana, who keeps a party boat in Miami. Saldana got approached by this dude from a company called NTJ Holdings, and they agreed to do some soap-and-water action in exchange for NTJ getting a kickback. Saldana, in return, gets a whole new conduit for the Blizzard for Entrada and his brothers, and they take over the Financial District. And who better to distribute the product than some inside folks? People who are at home in the Financial District? People who probably wouldn't be scrutinized too closely?"

"Like investment bankers?"

"Exactly."

Sebastian mulled this over. "That sounds good, but how can Saldana operate in New York without permission from the Mafia Families?"

"According to my ex, Saldana is on friendly terms with one of the underbosses in the Families, who put in a good word for him."

"Which means that this underboss is getting a piece of the action himself. You have been a busy boy."

"Yes, indeed," Zachary replied. "Especially since my ex is now feeling nostalgic, and will be flying to California for a work-related conference next month."

Sebastian shook his head. "That's on you, player. But for real, thanks for the info. It helps a lot."

"I'll catch you on the other side," Zachary said before he hung up.

~~~

Malcolm returned to the office a few hours later and dropped his briefcase off by his desk. He picked up the manila envelope that had been placed there by Alicia. Before he'd left the office, and after Jonathan and Sebastian left, he'd called Alicia and told her exactly what he needed, and when he needed it. He flipped through the papers, nodding to himself, then locked them in his bottom desk drawer. Malcolm strolled down the hall until he reached Trey's office. Trey was on the phone and looked up at Malcolm with surprise when he entered the office.

"I'll call you back," Trey said as he hung up the phone quickly. He turned back to his computer and wiggled the mouse on his mouse pad. "What do you want, Malcolm?"

Malcolm eased into one of the chairs that faced Trey's large chrome and glass desk as he regarded Nate's son. Trey wasn't necessarily a bad guy, and Malcolm had no personal beef with him, but he reminded Malcolm of a little kid who was constantly trying to get attention. "I just wanted to stop by and chat about this weird thing I found in our client database."

Trey continued to concentrate on his fantasy football team scores, even as the muscles in his back knotted up with tension. Malcolm didn't often come by his office. In fact, Trey could count on one hand the amount of times Malcolm had personally graced him with his presence, in all the years he'd been at Quasar. "Like what?"

"Like a slew of businesses that signed for swaps, and an extremely high LIBOR, only to terminate the deals six months to the day later."

Trey feigned surprise. "Really? That's wild." He moved his mouse around and clicked it. "So, where did you find this stuff, again?"

"In the client database, on the K drive." Malcolm watched Trey like a hawk. He silently gave the other man props for keeping his game face on. Trey was good, but Malcolm was better.

"What made you look there?" Trey immediately regretted that question.

Malcolm raised an eyebrow. "I was doing some research for an upcoming proposal I'm putting together." He regarded Trey. "The funny thing is, these companies were in a deal with a Quasar subsidiary called NTJ Holdings." A pause, then, "You know anything about that?"

A bead of sweat wended its way down Trey's spine. "Know about what?"

"NTJ Holdings. That name kept popping up in some of the accounts. As a matter of fact," Malcolm crossed one ankle over the opposite knee, displaying quietly patterned dress socks, "most of those accounts were assigned to you."

"That's crazy!" Trey exclaimed. "I don't know anything about NTJ Holdings."

"Really? Hmm." Malcolm looked around the office; the décor tried to give an impression of opulence and importance, but didn't quite make it. A red-and-gold patterned Oriental throw rug complemented the black suede sofa on one wall, and provided one of the few spots of color in the room. Silver trinkets from Tiffany were scattered about the office: clocks, cups, a pen-and-pencil desk set. The desk was larger than Malcolm's and was graced with a glass paperweight, in addition to a charging cradle for Trey's iPhone and a black and gold fraternity mug. A silver business card holder stood next to an incongruous green lava lamp perched near a corner of the desk. Behind the desk, and to Trey's left, was a miniature black refrigerator; to his right was a silver-studded black leather trunk that could double as extra seating. It was past the zone of "eclectic" and went straight into "confusing". Obviously, Trey chose not to enlist the services of the corporate interior designer.

"I like what you've done with the place. It's so...interesting." He ignored Trey's glower and got back to the matter at hand. "So you don't know anything about NTJ Holdings?"

"I just said that I didn't," Trey snapped. All pretense at ignoring Malcolm was abandoned as he clenched and unclenched his fists.

"But Landries Real Estate Group; that was your account, right? And Cauldrice Properties was Jeff's?" A slight smirk tugged at the corner of his lips. "You and Jeff like to tag team on accounts."

Trey waved an impatient hand. "Look, Malcolm, if you have a point to make, then make it."

"I already did," Malcolm said coldly. "Most of your accounts listed NTJ Holdings as an authorized party on the deals. Most of those deals were terminated, at the request of the client, on the sixtieth day. And," Malcolm stood and stared down at Trey. "On at least half of those accounts, Nigel had been assigned as the junior analyst. Yet he seemed clueless about some of the most general aspects of these deals, except for Cauldrice and Landries. So what's up?"

Trey snorted. "I don't know, Malcolm. I don't know what's up. But what I do know is that the next time you roll up on me with some bullshit conspiracy theories, you'd better be ready to back them up."

Malcolm shrugged. "I didn't know I was spinning bullshit conspiracy theories, but okay." He turned and walked to the door. With one hand on the doorknob, Malcolm turned back to Trey. "Oh, I forgot to mention one other thing. The company books are showing that payment was made to and by those accounts that listed NTJ Holdings as a subsidiary. However, those payments are not reconciling with the total operating budget." His stare was pointed. "That might bear some more looking into." Malcolm opened the door and walked out.

Trey stared at the now-empty doorway. Malcolm was the last person who needed to catch wind of things.

The question now was, what was Malcolm going to do? Would he go to Nate and tell him what Trey had done? Trey shook his head and quickly dismissed that idea. Malcolm liked to see his victims suffer; he wouldn't tell Nate anything right now, if ever. The thought of having something concrete to hold over Trey's head would be more satisfying to Malcolm than the more instant gratification of seeing Trey disgraced.

Trey dropped his head into his hands and cursed beneath his breath. What should he do now? He was so close. The scandal from Nigel's arrest would discourage potential investors from buying IPO stock in Quasar. Nigel, who was too curious for his own good, would take the fall and end up in a federal penitentiary. Malcolm would take some of the heat because he was the primary mentor and trainer for Nigel, and his frequent travels to Miami would place him under suspicion as well. With Malcolm's reputation tarnished and the company staying private, Trey could make his move and show his father that he wasn't such a screw-up after all. The clients he made during his swap scam had legitimate businesses that Quasar could take on. Everything had been going according to plan before the DEA began to look too closely. Why, Trey had no idea. He gave them a suspect and evidence on a silver platter. Slam dunk. So what happened?

Trey's numbered bank account in Switzerland had a healthy balance, and he was listed as the owner of some prime pieces of real estate in Brazil, the Caymans, and Spain. Malcolm had been correct about the discrepancies; due to the volume of some of the deals, payment had been made to NTJ by other methods than cash, with property being the preferred alternative. Payments to the other companies were made with firm funds. But still, Trey had buried such evidence so far in the system, it would take a very skilled person to dig it out. No one in IT had done it; Trey had a contact in IT who would have tipped him off if someone had come sniffing that way, the same contact who gave Trey access to employee passwords. Which meant that Malcolm had gotten someone outside of IT to do it, maybe even outside of the company. That would be the smart thing to do, and Malcolm was very smart.

Trey leaned back and stared at the ceiling. He was meeting a potential client the next day to discuss a deal; maybe this should be the last one. It may be time to cut his losses, at least until things died down and Malcolm got off his case. Trey picked up his phone and called Jeff. They had some things to discuss.

TEN

Tia, along with her cousins Tracey, Regina and Rachel, cruised the traffic-clogged streets near the Marcy Street Projects en route to the Scott home. The car and conversation was filled with both packages and chatter about their all-day shopping spree. As the car idled at a light, Regina's eyes roamed the narrow street. A lone figure caught her attention and she squinted to make sure she was seeing correctly. "Oi! Isn't that Priscilla?"

"Priscilla who?" Tracey craned her neck to see to whom Regina was referring.

"Nigel's wife."

Tia looked at Regina in the rearview mirror. "Why would Priscilla be around here, and at this time of evening?" She glanced at the clock in the dashboard. 8:46 p.m.

"I did see her. She's right there!" Regina pressed a manicured fingernail against the window. Rachel, who rode shotgun, peeked out of the passenger side window in the direction where the younger girl pointed. A slight figure in blue jeans and sneakers walked with her head down, a gray fleece pullover and orange scarf shielding her from the chilled evening air. She clutched a large black satchel bag to her body. "Spot her, Rachel?"

"That does look like Priscilla," Rachel agreed. "But Tia's right. Why would Pris be down here at this time of night? Who does she know around here? And where are the children?"

"It's probably just someone who looks like her," Tracey commented. "Priscilla wouldn't leave the babies to run the streets at night."

Tia honked her horn to get the woman's attention, but she had already turned the corner and disappeared.

"That was her," Regina insisted. "Maybe she's shagging a bloke on the side."

"Yeah, right," Tracey scoffed. "Priscilla ain't going nowhere. Nigel worships the ground she walks on."

"Everyone doesn't think like you, Regina," Rachel admonished. "I know it's a foreign concept, but there are people that love each other and don't stray. Like your parents."

"Whatever." Regina tossed her hair over her shoulders and shrugged. "Nigel may love Priscilla, but don't be too certain that the reverse is true. Her sort is always trying to trade up."

Tia shook her head as she turned onto Halsey Avenue. "You need a nap, Gina. Talking all that craziness."

"Mark my words," Regina said in a dire tone. "Priscilla bears watching."

~~~

Priscilla walked at a brisk pace and pulled her orange scarf tighter around the zippered neck of her gray fleece pullover. Her eyes darted around her, keeping a constant watch on her surroundings. She had never been in this area before, and she clutched her black satchel bag closer. The Marcy Avenue Projects was not a place to take a leisurely stroll in broad daylight, let

165

alone at night. But Trey asked--no, told her to make this delivery, as the recipient was unable to come into the city.

Priscilla walked through a maze of brick buildings until she came to the proper one. She removed her phone from her jeans pocket and checked the address on the GPS mapping app against the numbered sign on the building. She found the apartment she wanted on the building directory and dialed the corresponding digits. After a few rings, a disembodied voice growled through the speaker. "Yeah?"

"NTJ," Priscilla said, hoping that the quaver in her voice went unnoticed.

"10-C." Priscilla was buzzed in and walked across a surprisingly clean foyer, in red-trimmed, industrial beige tones, to the dark gray elevator doors. One was already waiting and Priscilla stepped inside. She pushed the button for the tenth floor and held her nose against the fetid odor of urine from the puddle in the opposite corner. On the tenth floor, she noted the numbering of the apartment doors and went left around the corner to a red-painted door with "10-C" in brass letters. Priscilla rapped on the door in a prearranged signal: two short raps, then three long raps, then two more short raps.

Priscilla wished she could make this delivery and get it over with; something about this building gave her the creeps. After what seemed like an eternity of clicks and clacks as the locks were being undone; the door swung open and Priscilla looked down at a heavyset man in an electric wheelchair. He looked Priscilla up and down, then reversed the wheelchair and drove down the narrow hall. Priscilla followed him past a small yet neat kitchen, and into the living room. The man wheeled around to face Priscilla. "You got the snow?"

The man's hungry brown gaze followed her every move as she retrieved a small glassine bag of an opalescent white substance from her satchel: Blizzard. From the corner of her eye. she noticed his large, meaty hand tighten around the joystick that maneuvered the wheelchair. Priscilla hefted the bag in her hand. "You got the money?"

A lecherous grin split his meaty face. He reached beneath the seat of his wheelchair and tugged until he removed a wrinkled brown paper back. Priscilla's skin crawled as one of his damp, sausage-like fingers brushed against her hand as she took the bag from him. She opened the bag and removed the stacks of crisp $100 bills, then quickly counted them twice before replacing them back in the bag. $5,000 for 2.5 ounces of Blizzard. Priscilla stuffed the money in her bag before handing the Blizzard over. This time, the man's finger deliberately grazed Priscilla's hand. She yanked her hand back and turned to leave, but was stopped by a heavy, sweaty hand on her arm.

"You ain't got to go right now, do you?" The man grinned wide enough to display a missing upper-right molar. His hand slid from Priscilla's arm down to his bulging crotch. "I got some more business for you to handle."

Priscilla could barely keep the disgust from her face. The man saw it and his grin took a nasty turn. He dangled the bag of Blizzard in front of her face. "I'll share."

Priscilla licked her lips, her eyes darting from the bag to the man's face. The craving had been under control but roared back with a vengeance. She clenched her jaw; she was determined not to whore herself any more than she had already. First with Nigel, then with Trey, and both for very good reasons. "No."

"You sure?" The man shook the bag to capture Priscilla's attention again. "I got something you want," he waggled his tongue at her, "and you got something I want. So why we can't help each other out?

"That wasn't part of the transaction," Priscilla said. The quaver had returned to her voice and she toughened her tone. "And if word gets back to NTJ that you were short on your money, you won't get anything else."

"Short on my money?" The grin fell away. "I gave you the exact amount! How you gon' say I'm short?"

"Because I have the money right now," Priscilla replied in a cold tone. "Leave me alone, or it will be short by the time I turn it in."

"Fuck you, you skank snowhead bitch," the man fumed. "Get the fuck outta here!"

Priscilla turned to leave, the man still spewing invectives to her back. As she headed toward the subway, tears once again sprang to her eyes. How had she come to this? She had never done drugs in her life, had never even smoked a cigarette. Then she'd met Trey at the company picnic. Later on, she'd stumbled into a room where Trey was laying out lines of white powder for some of the younger executives. Instead of sending her away, he invited her in. Trey explained what the Blizzard was, that it was better than plain cocaine, and gave you a high followed by a mellowed-out buzz. Priscilla, overwhelmed by Nigel's expectations of her as a wife and by dealing with two children under the age of three on a full-time basis, gladly took the first descent into hell.

It was incredible. Trey, however, failed to mention that Blizzard not only provided a better high, but it was also more addictive. Priscilla quickly depleted her and Nigel's joint savings to buy the drug as her habit increased. When Nigel began to ask too many questions, Trey offered her a way to make money and finance her habit at a discount. She made drug runs for him to other clients in Brooklyn. When her habit became too large in so short a time, she began to trade sex with Trey for Blizzard. She kept Nigel satisfied with oral and hand jobs, but they'd not had traditional intercourse since Miles was born. The one thing she hadn't done was touch her personal nest egg of $150,000. That was her escape money, and she had to hold onto it at all costs.

Priscilla caught sight of herself in the plate glass window of a shop. Her eyes were gaunt and shadowed, her nose red and runny from the cold. She'd forgotten her hat at home, and her lifeless, dark brown hair was mussed around her face by the wind. Priscilla noticed the dejected set of her shoulders and a tear finally escaped. How had her life come to this?

~ ~ ~

Tia, Rachel, Regina and Tracey joined the rest of the family in the basement of the Scott home. The arrival of other cousins, friends, and associates from within the five boroughs stopped by for good times and better food. The makeshift dance floor in the center of the room was now crowded with young bodies grooving to an eclectic mix of Top 40 and old-school R&B, rap, soca, and calypso. Rachel, Regina and Tracey went elsewhere while Tia approached the corner where Sebastian, Jonathan, Alex, Dante, and Trackie were holding court with one of the recent arrivals. She squealed with delight as she rushed toward Philip Pierre, Trackie's older brother and a law student at Duke University. "Phil! When did you get in?"

Philip rose and hugged his cousin, his gray eyes gleaming. "I got in a few hours ago. Sam flew into Raleigh-Durham from Miami; I met here there, and we drove up." He nodded at an adjacent corner where his sister, Samantha, was talking and laughing with Regina, Rachel and Tracey, who was holding her and Kenneth's toddler daughter, Nancey.

"How's law school? And how are you liking North Carolina?"

Philip shrugged. "It's okay. The people are really nice and they speak to each other, even to perfect strangers. It's slower down there and there are no subways, but the food is good. Lots of trees and grass, too." He grinned. "As for law school, it is what it is. Can't say that I'd want to repeat the experience again. Thanks for that book you bought me, though. Scott Turow was on the money, even though he wrote the book about his law school experience back in the sixties."

"Yeah, everyone I knew in the legal profession said that *One L* was a very accurate account of your first year."

Philip looked around and when he didn't spot Nigel, lowered his voice. "Speaking of law, what is this madness with Nigel? He was arrested for drugs?"

Tia nodded and replied, "He was arrested. His guilt remains to be seen, though it doesn't look good. Mum has ordered Sebastian to look into it from the DEA side, even though he's supposed to be on vacation."

"DEA?" Philip's eyes widened. "Federal? Jesus Christ." He shook his head and looked at Sebastian. "How much did they find on him?"

"Eight keys," Sebastian said. Philip's mouth dropped open.

"He was set up," Dante added. "And, thanks to Trackie and Jon, we think we found out why."

Philip looked at his brother. "Were you hacking again?"

"Who, me?" Trackie's expression was innocent even as his gray eyes danced with laughter.

"Cut the crap, Trackie," Philip laughed. "I remember when you reconfigured my hard drive and erased some files, after I spilled chili on that shirt I borrowed from you." Trackie was a year younger than Phillip and the two were rather close, as they were with all their siblings.
"I didn't erase them," Trackie protested. "I just moved them somewhere else on your hard drive. And you got them back."

"After I personally took you to the mall and let you select a new shirt, which I had to pay for."

Trackie shrugged. "I wanted to wear that shirt on a date. You were messing up my flow."

"Whatever. You were twelve years old, you didn't have a flow, and you were meeting your friends in the food court at the mall." Philip turned to Sebastian. "Anyway, has there been any progress?"

"I guess. But I'm not officially investigating anything, so I don't know much."

Philip nodded. "How is Nigel holding up?"

"He's actually hanging in there. Didn't know he had it in him. I figured he'd be weeping into Aunt Lisa's skirts by now," Jonathan commented.

"Nothing like an indictment to make you man up," Alex smirked.

"Stop that," Tia scolded. "Now is not the time to pick on Nigel."

"If not now, when? If not us, who?" Dante grinned as Tia shot him a black look. The others broke out in laughter.

Philip took another look around the room. "How's Priscilla? I don't see her here."

Tia looked around in surprise. "She's not here? She must be out still running her errand, then." At the confused looks she explained, "Regina thinks she saw Priscilla out by the Marcy Projects, on our way home."

Dante looked at his watch. "At this time of night?"

"What the hell was Priscilla doing out by Marcy?" Alex demanded. "She ain't got no place being over there."

"Are you sure it was Priscilla?" Sebastian asked Tia with a frown.

"I didn't see her very well, because I was driving. Regina, Rachel and Tracey did, though."

Jonathan looked at his cousins in confusion. "What is this Marcy place?"

"Marcy Projects," Dante replied. "Home of the rapper Jay-Z. Kinda rough area, like most of Bushwick used to be, or the West End in London."

"Projects?" Jonathan frowned. "You mean, government-subsidized housing?"

The group broke into laughter. "Yeah," Dante said, chuckling.

"Whom would Priscilla know of over there?" Trackie wondered aloud.

Philip pulled at his bottom lip thoughtfully. "I agree with Sebastian. Are you sure that it was indeed Priscilla that you saw? You know how Regina likes to exaggerate."

"True, but Tracey and Rachel agreed with her," Tia said. "I'm more inclined to trust their judgment."

Conversation paused as Nigel entered the room and approached the group. "Hey guys," he said as his gaze roved over his cousins' faces. "What's up?" He looked at Philip and smiled. "Hey, Phil! When did you get here? Did Samantha come too?"

Philip rose and hugged Nigel. He was one of the few male cousins who actually got along with Nigel. "We drove up from Philly a few hours ago. Sam's over there with Rachel, Regina and Tracey." He sat back down as Nigel continued to stand. "Where you been?"

"I took the kids to the park, then out for ice cream. Priscilla's taking a class down at Long Island University tonight."

Nigel seemed oblivious to the confused silence that his statement generated.

"Really?" Jonathan inquired with a bland expression. "What type of class?"

"Crocheting, or knitting, or something," Nigel explained. "It meets on Tuesdays and Thursday evenings, seven to eight-thirty. Pris is really good at making things; she even sewed all the curtains in our apartment. She's going to go into business for herself and sell what she makes. Handcrafted items are popular these days."

The cousins nodded, playing along with Nigel's delusion. "Good for her," Dante said. "Entrepreneurship is the name of the game these days."

"Yep," Nigel agreed. "And she can work from home, so that she can still be with the kids. She's happy about that." A faint buzzing sound from Nigel's pocket caught his attention. He pulled out his cell phone, and his face lit up at the display. "Excuse me," he said as he did a hasty about-face. The cousins watched Nigel murmur into the phone as he sought a quiet place.

"I thought you said you just saw her over by Marcy?" Dante hissed to Tia. She held out her hands in a helpless gesture.

"Wonder who was on the phone to put that pep in Nigel's step?" Alex inquired.

"I've never seen Nigel move that fast," Philip remarked.

"I know, right?" Dante said. "He was moving like his ass was on fire."

"Yeah," Sebastian agreed as he stared after Nigel with interest.

"Maybe it's a woman," Tia commented.

Sebastian's mind flashed back to the earlier visit to Quasar, and the curious looks given to him by the receptionist. Tia might have been onto something.

The men snorted and sucked their teeth. "What?" Tia asked with a smile. "Why couldn't it be a woman?"

"Besides the fact that Priscilla would kill him?" Jonathan asked.

Dante wrinkled his nose. "Who else would want him but Priscilla, and I still haven't figured that out."

"Ah, you never know, D," Tia teased. "Women are attracted to more intangible things than men are. Nigel might be throwing out some vibes that you all aren't aware of."

175

"Eww." Dante shuddered. "Nigel picking up women is not a visual I want in my head."

"Get off Nigel, now," Philip defended. "He's not a bad-looking guy. He's a Pierre, after all."

"You're quite right, Philip." Jonathan licked a finger and smoothed down an eyebrow. "The Pierre lot has some handsome blokes."

"Definitely," Dante grinned as he stuck out his chest.

"No doubt," Sebastian agreed.

Tia shrugged. "Y'all look a'ight." Her comment caused the group to burst into laughter again.

"You'd better look again," Philip shot back. He puffed out his chest. "I am a man, baby. All man."

Tia held her hand up, palm facing Philip. "Whatever, Philip. I used to baby-sit you, so don't even go there."

As the cousins continued their good-natured ribbing, Nigel stepped into a walk-in utility closet and shut the door behind him. "Okay, I'm back," he spoke into the cell phone.

"How have you been?" Assata asked. "I've been so worried about you. And I couldn't call you, and your cousin came by, and..."

"Whoa, whoa," Nigel interrupted her. "My cousin?"

"Yeah, Sebastian Scott? The DEA agent. He was with a Jonathan Heath," Assata explained. "They met with Malcolm."

"Jonathan is my cousin too. His mother, Sebastian's mother, and my father are all siblings." Nigel's brow furrowed. "I wonder if they talked to Malcolm about me?"

"Well, whatever they said to Malcolm must not have been good, because he had a major attitude after they left." Assata lowered her voice. "And I heard him ask Alicia to try and get Trey's calendar info for the past six months."

Nigel felt a twinge of anxiety. Why didn't either Sebastian or Jonathan tell him that they'd gone up to Quasar? What did they say to Malcolm? What was going on? He put his worries aside and focused on the joy of talking to Assata. "I miss you," Nigel said softly.

"I miss you too," Assata replied. "I wish we could see each other. It's been over a week."

"I know. Trey had me doing on a lot of busywork before...." Nigel burst into a cold sweat at the memories of his brief incarceration, and pushed them aside. "What are you doing now?"

"Now? Nothing much, just trying to figure out what to eat for dinner."

"Can I come over?"

"Can you get away?" Assata's voice was excited.

"Yeah. We got a bunch of family and friends here, dancing and socializing. They won't miss me for a couple of hours."

"Okay. I'll make us something to eat."

"Cool. See you soon." Nigel paused. "I love you, Assata."

"I love you, too."

Nigel tucked his phone back into his pocket and slid out of the closet. He took a quick look around: no one was in the immediate vicinity. He took a roundabout way to the front door--upstairs, through the den, then the family room, grabbing his fleece jacket en route. He managed to escape detection as he left the house with a spring in his step.

ELEVEN

Sebastian let the conversation flow around him as he thought about Nigel's recent comments regarding Priscilla's absence. His mind went back to the night of Nigel's arrest and Priscilla's reaction. Now, Priscilla had been spotted in a seedy part of Brooklyn, alone, at night, and had apparently lied to Nigel about where she was. Could Priscilla be involved in Nigel's arrest? The question of how the Blizzard got into Nigel's office still hadn't been answered, and Nigel claimed that no strangers had been in his office without his knowledge. But what about his wife? Then, there was the matter of whomever Nigel had been speaking with on the phone. Whoever it was, Nigel wanted to keep their identity secret. But why? Sebastian rose from the couch.

He looked around the room for his mother, and found her in a corner, deep in conversation with his grandmother, her sister, and some neighbors. He approached the group with trepidation; he was very much afraid that his marital status and lack of children would be an immediate topic of interrogation. "Excuse me, ladies," he started.

"Hello, Sebastian," the group chimed, almost as one, to cut him off. Sebastian gave a sheepish wave.

"So handsome, my grandson," Nana Pierre beamed.

"Yes, he is," one of the neighbors concurred. "And got a good job. When you gettin' married, eh? Make you mudda some pickney dem?"

Sebastian tried not to show his panic at his fears coming true. He pasted a social grin on his face and turned to his mother. "Mom, can I speak with you for a moment?"

"Of course. Excuse me," Janelle said to the group as she followed her son out of the room. He led her down the hall to her office and turned on the light. "What's going on, Sebastian?"

"Have a seat for a minute, Mom." He gestured to the couch adjacent to her desk, which she kept for those patients who took the "on the couch" metaphor for psychotherapy, literally. At his mother's expectant look, he asked, "Mom, how much do you know about Nigel's finances? And before you deny that you know anything," he held up a hand to stay her protest, "I know that you and your brothers and sisters talk: not just to each other, but about each other. So, what do you know?"

Janelle closed her mouth and nodded. "You're right," she sighed. "We do talk. And what I can tell you is that Nigel is not that good with money. Even though he doesn't make all that much at his job, he makes enough to where he should take care of his family. Plus, his dividends from Pierre International should have given him a cushion. He borrows money from Joseph, and he tells them they are saving for a house, but..." She shook her head in disbelief. "Anyway, Priscilla stays at home with the children, so that is a factor as well--although they are saving a lot of money on daycare, and they don't have a car to maintain." She looked at her firstborn. "Why?"

"Just trying to figure out a motive. Money is usually a big part of why people get into drug trafficking in the first place."

"Hmm." She pursed her lips as she debated upon sharing additional information. "There have also been rumors that Nigel gambles." At Sebastian's surprised expression, she added, "Nothing big. A football game, lottery tickets. Things like that. He may lose up to a hundred dollars or so on a sports game, but he's not at a point to where he's dealing with loan sharks. He has that much sense, at least."

Sebastian sighed. His cousin was quite the chameleon, it seemed. "Alright. Thanks a lot, Mom. If you think of anything else, or hear anything else, please let me know. Don't forget, I fly out in a couple of days and I can't do much of anything when I'm gone."

"I know, and I appreciate you helping Nigel, even though I know you hate it."

"Mom..." Sebastian had the grace to look embarrassed.

Janelle chuckled. "I pushed you into this, and I know that you and Nigel have never gotten along, not since you were children. Some of that is due to some things between me and your uncle Joseph that happened long before you were born. Some of that is just Nigel wanting to be like you, and failing." She pushed to her feet with an exhausted sigh. "But, that is part and parcel of being a family." She rubbed her lower back. "I should probably replace that couch, but I'm quite fond of it."

"Plus, it keeps your patients from getting too comfortable," Sebastian teased as he slung an arm across her shoulder.

"No comment," Janelle grinned. As they went back down the hall, she asked, "Sebastian, I think we may need more napkins. Your father bought a big pack earlier today. Can you go upstairs and get it, please? It's in the kitchen, on top of the refrigerator."

"Sure." Janelle continued down the hall to the party while Sebastian went upstairs to the kitchen. He was on his way back downstairs with the bulk package of napkins when he heard the front door open. Priscilla walked in with a runny nose and flushed cheeks. "Hey, Pris."

Priscilla jumped at the sound of Sebastian's voice. "Uh, hi, Sebastian." She set her satchel on the ground and unwound the bright orange scarf from around her neck. "I didn't see you there."

Sebastian looked at his watch. "We were wondering where you were. We were getting worried."

"Yeah, well, I had to run some errands. " She sniffled and wiped her nose with the back of her hand.

He shifted the napkins beneath one arm. "Catching a cold?"

"Yeah." Priscilla gave a weak grin. "Must've caught it from one of the kids."

Sebastian nodded. He looked her up and down with an appraising eye. Priscilla's cheeks were more gaunt than he remembered, but that could be attributed to

182

stress over Nigel's situation. Her nose was running, but that could be attributed to the evening chill. She wore a scarf, but no hat on her head. The fleece jacket hung down over denim-clad hips and legs; the jeans seemed to be a bit baggy for her frame. Suspicion loomed in Sebastian's mind, was squashed, then raised its ugly head again. Was Priscilla using?

Sebastian leaned against the newel post in a deceptively casual manner. "Where's Nigel?"

Priscilla shrugged, then removed her fleece jacket. The black turtleneck she wore beneath it accented her thinness. "Isn't he here?"

"No. The aunts are in the kitchen with my mom and Nana, the men are in the den with my dad and Papa, and the cousins are downstairs in the basement. The kids are down there too."

"Oh. Well, I don't know." She retrieved the satchel and slung it onto her shoulder. Priscilla shifted her body first in the direction of the kitchen, then in the direction of the basement, as if unsure of where to go. She held the satchel close to her body and noticed Sebastian's eyes narrow at the tightening of her hands around the straps. "I, uh, gotta use the bathroom. I'll see you downstairs." Priscilla hurried past Sebastian, feeling his eyes on her back.

Once in the bathroom, Priscilla placed the bag on the counter and rested her hands on the sink. She looked at her reflection in the mirror and frowned at how messy she looked The interaction with the wheelchair-bound man, combined with the not-so-subtle interrogation from Sebastian, had further frazzled her nerves. She reached into her tote, moved the money-filled paper bag aside, and removed a gold-tone plastic lipstick tube. She removed the cap and dipped in her pinkie, coming up with a healthy scoop of Blizzard. She snorted first up one nostril, then the other.

A few minutes later, the Blizzard took effect. Priscilla felt revved up, yet smoothed out, which was just what the Blizzard was supposed to do. It made users feel like they were out in a, well, a blizzard. The cold perked you up while the snow fell and blanketed sound and senses. Priscilla replaced the lipstick tube in her bag and pulled out a hairbrush and comb. She fixed her hair, applied lip gloss, adjusted her clothing and took a final look at herself in the mirror. Gone was the tiredness and runny nose. Now her dark brown eyes sparkled and she looked energized and ready to socialize. And as for Sebastian, well, she'd have to be more careful in his presence.

~~~

A few hours later, the fête was still going strong. Janelle and her sisters and sisters-in-law brought down massive quantities of food, in addition to that which was brought by friends and neighbors. The music continued to blare and everyone socialized, danced, and enjoyed each other's company. Papa Pierre had somehow managed to find cases of Vat No. 19 and Angostura 1919 Trinidadian rums in Queens, which added to the festivities. Sebastian spotted Nigel sitting in a corner, alone, nursing a Carib. He walked over and sat next to his cousin. "What's up, Nigel? You disappeared on us. Where did you go?"

"I, uh, just wanted to get out for a bit." A flush worked its way up Nigel's neck as he fidgeted with the beer bottle in his hands. "I took a walk."

Sebastian once again thought of Tia's words, and both Priscilla's and Nigel's behaviors. "Why are you over here by yourself?"

Nigel gave a tired smile. "Being the family celebrity can wear on you. Seeing the pity makes it worse."

Sebastian mentally agreed with Nigel. He took a deep breath and plunged in. "Nigel, I have to ask you some more unpleasant questions."

Nigel took a sip of beer as he stared at Sebastian. "How unpleasant?"

"Very."

Nigel rolled the bottle between his palms, his eyes on the motion. "Will it help end this nightmare?"

Sebastian didn't want to tell him that if he was on the right track, the nightmare would get worse. "I hope so."

Nigel nodded. "Okay, then." He looked around the crowded room. "You wanna talk here?"

"Nope. Too many people. Let's go upstairs." Sebastian and Nigel walked around the perimeter of the crowd and upstairs. Sebastian heard booming laughter from behind the den door, and voices in the living room, so he led Nigel upstairs to his bedroom. "Have a seat." Sebastian gestured to the bed. He closed and locked the door before taking a seat in an adjacent chair. Nigel's face was pinched, and he held his thin body as if anticipating a blow. Sebastian leaned back and prayed for strength before he began. "Nigel, remember when I asked you if any strangers had been in your office recently, the day you were arrested?"

Nigel nodded. "Yeah, and I told you that there hadn't been."

"Okay." Sebastian paused, trying to figure out the best way to ask his next question. "Did Priscilla visit you at the office?"

"Yeah," Nigel replied. "She stopped by that morning to bring me my lunch. I'd forgotten it that morning when I left for work." He frowned. "Why?"

Sebastian held up a hand in warning. "Just bear with me for a minute. Did she visit you often at work?"

"Sometimes. She might meet me with the kids for lunch when I could get away, or she'd bring me dinner if I had to work late." His frown deepened. "Surely you don't think that Priscilla has anything to do with this?"

"She had access to your cubicle, Nigel. Nobody would think twice of seeing her there."

"She's my wife!"

"I can't rule her out."

"She's my wife." Nigel enunciated each word with cold precision. A stubborn look crossed his face.

Sebastian knew what that look meant, but he had to press on nonetheless. "Where was Pris earlier tonight?"

"What do you mean? I told you, she was at her crocheting class at LIU."

"Really?" Sebastian examined Nigel's face. "I saw her when she came in tonight. She told me she was running errands."

Nigel waved a hand in dismissal. "So she ran some errands either before or after her class. Big deal! I won't have you trying to get Priscilla mixed up in this madness."

"Is Priscilla using drugs, Nigel?"

"Now that's enough!" Nigel rose, jaw clenched, fists clenched at his sides. He wore an impressive scowl. "I don't like what you're trying to say, Sebastian, so you'd best stop it right now."

"Has she been sick, Nigel? Had a runny nose? Lost weight?"

Nigel's posture relaxed a bit in surprise. "She had a bit of a cold. She caught it from the kids."

Sebastian felt a wave of pity for his cousin. "The kids didn't look sick the other day. They don't look sick now."
"They're fine. Priscilla has the cold now. It's affected her appetite, as has this...court thing." Nigel's eyes narrowed. "That's all it is. Stress and illness. It's enough to make anybody sick. Now, I'd advise you to drop this conspiracy theory, Sebastian. Priscilla shouldn't be part of whatever sick idea is in your head." He strode to the door, unlocked it, and stormed out. Sebastian heard him stomping down the stairs.
He sighed and leaned back in the chair with closed

eyes. All things considered, he thought their talk went well.

TWELVE

The next morning, Sebastian called the offices of Quasar.

"Quasar Financial. Assata speaking. How may I help you?"

"Assata, this is Sebastian Scott. I was there yesterday with another man, to see Malcolm Jennings."

"Oh," Assata said in surprise. "Hello. I remember you."

"I need to ask you some questions, if you don't mind."

"Why?"

"This is related to the Nigel Pierre case."

"I, uh..." Assata stammered. "Um, okay." Panic lay in the background of her voice, threatening to erupt. "Are you coming back here?"

"Actually, I think it's best if we meet away from the office. It won't take long, I promise you."

Assata was silent for a moment. "I normally take my lunch break around 12:30, but it might be better for me to take a late lunch. I could meet you somewhere." She named a seafood restaurant about five blocks from the office.

"That's fine," Sebastian agreed. "I'll see you there around 2:30. If you're late, I'll wait for you."

"Thank you for calling Quasar," Assata said in a suddenly formal tone before a dial tone sounded in Sebastian's ear.

Sebastian walked into A Taste of the Sea at 2:15 pm.

He looked around and noticed that most of the traffic was for takeout; quite a few of the blue-draped tables in the room were unoccupied. The interior was pleasantly dim and was accented by long tanks of fish and lobster. There was one other couple in the far back corner of the room, kissing to the exclusion of everything and everyone else. Sebastian spared them a glance and curled his lip in disgust. He wasn't a fan of excessive public displays of affection.

At 2:32, Assata rushed through the doorway and looked for Sebastian. She walked over to the table and sat down, bumping against the table in her haste. She was clearly nervous; she fiddled with the buttons on her rust-colored cardigan sweater, smoothed her hands down her rust-and-brown paisley print skirt, played with the silverware. Sebastian tried to set her mind at ease. "Thank you for meeting me, Assata."

"No problem." She rearranged the sugar packets in the small dish on the table.

Sebastian watched the woman's movements. "Okay, Assata. Why are you so nervous?"

"I'm not nervous." Assata picked up the complimentary glass of water and sloshed some on the table, which she hastily mopped up with a paper napkin. She finally raised her eyes and met Sebastian's gaze. "Okay, maybe I'm a bit nervous."

"I can see that," Sebastian smiled. He was rewarded with a timid smile. "The question now becomes, why? I don't bite."

"That's not what I heard," Assata blurted out. At Sebastian's surprised look she added, "Whatever happened in your meeting with Malcolm yesterday, put him in a bad mood. He doesn't usually let that happen. He was especially taken aback by you guys being Nigel's cousins; it put him in an awkward position."

Sebastian cocked his head curiously. "How did you know that we were Nigel's cousins?" At her flush of embarrassment at saying too much, he asked, "Did Nigel tell you that?"

Assata hesitated, then nodded. "Nigel has talked about you. Quite a bit, in fact. His super-smart cousin who's a tough DEA agent in California. I think he's afraid of you, even as he admires you. He admires your cousin Jonathan, too. He's this big-shot international banker. I knew he had to be, because Malcolm wouldn't have given him the time of day if he weren't. He would have sent one of the junior partners, or a senior analyst, to speak with you. " She opened the menu and stared down at it, unseeing.

"Do you talk to Nigel a lot?

Another nod. "Yes."

"Outside of work?"

Assata took a deep breath and let it out slowly before nodding. "Yes." Her voice was still soft but stronger.

"Nigel and I, well...we've been...seeing each other, away from Quasar."

Sebastian made a mental note to listen to his sister more often. "How long has this been going on?"

Assata swallowed. "About four months or so." She traced a finger over the damp, wadded napkin. "We...at least, I...well, we're in love."

Sebastian blinked. "Nigel's married. With two young children."

"I know that. And I'm not proud of being involved with a married man. But we didn't plan it at all." Assata was silent as the waiter came to take their orders. Once he'd left, she continued. "Plus, he said he'd leave his wife once he'd made arrangements for child custody and visitation." Seeing Sebastian's skeptical expression she said, "I know it's sounds totally cliché, but this time it's true. Nigel had already drawn up the divorce papers and showed them to me. He was going to have them served on his wife."

Assata's comment reawakened Sebastian's suspicions of Priscilla. If what Assata said was true, then Priscilla had a motive for Nigel being in jail. "Did you see him last night?"

"Yes. He was at a big party your family was throwing. He slipped out and came to see me, then he went back to the party a few hours later."

Sebastian remembered the phone call that Nigel received and his disappearing act. "Okay. So you and Nigel are having an affair. That's really none of my business, unless it has a direct impact on this case. Does it?"

"I don't know," Assata replied. "Nigel didn't really talk to me about his work much, except..."

"Except what?" Sebastian asked as the platters of hot food were placed in front of them. Sebastian said a quick grace and munched on a French fry.

Assata stirred her clam chowder slowly. "Well, Nigel seemed very preoccupied the past few weeks. I thought it had been because he'd been traveling to Miami with Malcolm on a deal they were working on. But when I asked him about it, he said that Malcolm was the least of his worries. I tried to get more information out of him, but he just said that he was gathering his facts and when he got them all straight, he'd let me know."

Sebastian nodded and chewed. So far, Assata hadn't told him anything earth-shattering that would get Nigel off the hook. Time to try a different tack. "How did Nigel get along with his co-workers?"

Assata's smile was genuine for the first time since she'd walked into the restaurant. "He's your cousin. You should be able to figure that out. He is..." Assata waved a hand, trying to find the right words. "He's different. Nigel, as you know, has a very gentle spirit. I personally think that investment banking is not the proper place for him, but who am I to judge? We all do what we have to do." She ate a spoonful of chowder. "Anyway, he didn't--doesn't--have the cutthroat mentality that most bankers have. Which is why I was surprised, at first, when he was hired. But I later found out why he was really hired."

"And why was that?" Sebastian bit into his fish sandwich and wiped away a blob of tartar sauce from the corner of his mouth.

"His--your family. Pierre International."

Sebastian was impressed. Assata was a lot sharper than one might think. "And what is it about the company that's so important?"

Assata opened a packet of oyster crackers and sprinkled a few into her soup. "International connections. Everyone knows that Nate Jacobson wants to take Quasar public next year. It's also common knowledge, especially within the company, that Nate wants Quasar to have more of an international presence. Pierre International, through Nigel, would be a good starting point."

Score one for Jonathan. "But why PI? Surely there are other companies he'd considered?"

Assata nodded, her mouth full of food. "There still are," she said after swallowing. "But PI is small enough to be approachable, yet wildly profitable. Nate appreciates the family dynamic that drives the company, as it's similar to the one he employs at Quasar. Plus, I think that Nate's grandfather is from Tobago, or something like that."

Sebastian eyed Assata with an increasing respect. "Why aren't you in the back offices, closing deals yourself?"

Assata's eyes glowed with appreciation of the compliment. "Because my mother is ill and I'm taking care of her, and Quasar pays me very well and offers great benefits, with relatively little stress." She eyed Sebastian over the eye of her water glass. "Like I said before, we all do what we have to do."

Sebastian nodded as he popped the last of his sandwich into his mouth. "Back to the co-workers. Was there anyone that Nigel absolutely didn't get along with?"

Assata spooned chowder into her mouth as she paused to think. "Not really. Of course, Trey treated him like crap, but that's to be expected. He treats everyone that way, except Malcolm. Malcolm treats him like crap right back."

"Trey Jacobson?"

"Yeah. He's Nate's son."

"What's Trey's issue, both with other people and with Malcolm?"

Assata rested her spoon in the now-empty chowder bowl. "Trey is a typical spoiled only child. He gets off on being Nate's son, although everyone knows that Nate is very disappointed in Trey. He'd hoped that Trey would take the business a bit more seriously. That's why Trey and Malcolm get into it so much. Malcolm acts like Trey should: he's into the business, has Nate's back on a lot of things, handles the headaches so that Nate can tend to the migraines. And Trey hates that. He hates everything that Malcolm is about, because he deep down he wants to be Malcolm. You know?"

195

"Hmm." Sebastian chewed a mouthful of cole slaw. "And how does Trey feel about this IPO deal?"

Assata's brow furrowed. "Now that's interesting, that you'd bring that up. Everyone has been waiting for Trey to flip out as the date draws nearer, but he's been really upbeat. Like he could care less, and that's not like Trey. And he's been hanging around with Jeff Nixon more than usual, too. Although it's not unusual to see those two together; Jeff has always followed Trey around, even when they were in undergrad."

"Did you attend the same college as Jeff and Trey?"

Assata nodded. "And Malcolm. We were all at Drexel University at the same time, though we ran in completely different circles. I was in the artsy crowd, big surprise." She grinned, displaying even white teeth with a slight gap in the middle. "Trey and Jeff were deep into the fraternity life, and Malcolm kind of just did his own thing, even though he was in a different fraternity." She stopped, considering. "This probably won't mean anything to you, but I do remember a rumor going around, for a minute, that Malcolm wouldn't graduate due to a failed elective or something. But no one could really confirm it. I don't recall seeing him at graduation, but he was a business major and I was a liberal arts major, so I didn't think anything of it."

Sebastian filed that piece of information away for future reference. It could be easily checked, if need be. "Assata, I'm going to ask you what may seem like an odd question." He hesitated; asking the mistress about the wife seemed weird. "Have you ever seen Nigel's wife, Priscilla, at Quasar?"

Assata stiffened at the mention of Priscilla's name, then her shoulders deflated. "Yes, and no. Nigel brought her to the major company events, like the annual picnic and the Christmas party. And a few times she came to the office to bring him his lunch, or something that he'd left at home." She hesitated, then said, "Once, I saw her talking to Trey at the company picnic. They were deep in conversation. Weird, because I didn't know she even knew Trey. Nigel had never really worked with him, since Nate initially gave Malcolm the job of training Nigel."

"So they looked like they knew each other?" Sebastian tried to quell his excitement. This was the thread he was looking for.

"Well, I wouldn't say that much," Assata amended. "More like they were very comfortable with each other. Or rather, that they clicked off the bat. I noticed because Nigel was not as relaxed around the other Quasar people, but his wife blended in." Assata looked down at the table. "She's very pretty. Cold, but pretty."

Sebastian considered Assata's comment. "I agree on both counts, but you're just as pretty."

"Well, thank you, Sebastian." Assata's smile bloomed. "You're not bad, yourself."

Sebastian signaled for the check. As he waited for the waiter to return with his credit card and receipt, Sebastian looked around the room once more. His gaze again returned to the kissing couple he'd seen when he'd arrived. This time, the couple managed to come up for air, which gave Sebastian enough time to see that the man was Malcolm Jennings.

Assata had obviously seen Malcolm as well, because she whispered, "Oh my God, that's Malcolm!" Her tone turned disapproving. "And that's not his girlfriend, Mia."

Sebastian shot Assata a look; she wasn't exactly in a position to judge others, but he let that ride.

The woman peeled herself away from Malcolm and rose to walk to the restrooms at the rear of the restaurant. Sebastian took advantage of her absence. "Excuse me for a moment," he murmured to Assata as he walked over to Malcolm's table.

Malcolm was wiping his mouth and cheeks with a napkin when Sebastian approached. Surprise flashed across Malcolm's face, only to be replaced with irritation. "Yes?"

Sebastian stood in front of Malcolm, hands in his pockets. "Late lunch, Mr. Jennings?"

Malcolm looked Sebastian up and down, then looked over and saw Assata sitting at the table, looking at both of them. "Well, well. Our little Assata has certainly been a busy bee. Still waters run deep." He looked down at the traces of lipstick left on the napkin and scowled before balling it up and tossing it onto his half-empty plate. "I always thought her interests lay elsewhere."

Sebastian sat down, uninvited. "Let's talk, Mr. Jennings. I have some questions about some of your people at Quasar."

"I've been advised not to speak to you outside of the presence of my attorney." His tone was deceptively bland. "You can make an appointment with Ruth through my executive assistant."

Sebastian leaned closer and lowered his voice. "I don't have time to have a pissing contest with you, Jennings. I need some information, and I need it now."

Malcolm raised an eyebrow. "I don't have to tell you anything, and I've probably already said more than I should. You're not even supposed to be working on Nigel's case. Conflict of interest, isn't it, him being your cousin and all?" He leaned back in his seat. "There's no reason why I should talk to you."

"You know, that woman you're with looks nothing like the woman in the picture on your desk. Mia, I think her name is?" Sebastian smiled as he saw the flush rise up Malcolm's neck.

Malcolm poked his tongue in his cheek, then inclined his head in acquiescence. "Touché, Special Agent Scott." He noticed Jessica coming out of the restroom. "This isn't the best time to talk."

"Then when is the best time? Like I said, I don't have much of it to spare."

"I'm on my way back to the office. Be there in half an hour, or you'll get nothing." He smirked. "Like you, I don't have much time to spare."

Sebastian nodded, then went back to Assata. Assata's eyes were wide as she stared at Malcolm, then back at Sebastian. "What was that all about?"

Sebastian signed the receipt and tucked his credit card back into his wallet. "Nigel."

~~~

Twenty-five minutes later, Sebastian was in the lobby of Quasar. Assata had returned to her post in the reception area and had paged Alicia, Malcolm's executive assistant. To Sebastian's surprise, Alicia appeared within minutes of Assata's call and ushered him back to Malcolm's office; she didn't even blink at Sebastian's casual attire of jeans and a long-sleeved, lightweight navy blue sweater.

Malcolm rose when Sebastian entered. "Have a seat," Malcolm instructed. Alicia left silently, closing the door behind her.

Sebastian sat and Malcolm did the same. The two men regarded each other, much like two dogs. Sebastian understood that this was yet another power play; the person who spoke first, lost ground. However, since Sebastian was the one seeking answers, he didn't lose anything by speaking first. Plus, he figured that massaging Malcolm's ego would get him the answers he needed a lot faster. "Thank you for making time this afternoon, Mr. Jennings. I really appreciate it."

"You do that very well," Malcolm commented.

"Do what well?"

"Say the appropriate thing, but in a tone that invites me to go to hell." A smile tugged at the corner of Malcolm's lips. At Sebastian's shrug, the smile became full-fledged, displaying even white teeth and crinkles around his eyes. "I like you, Scott. God knows why. And you can call me Malcolm." He leaned back in his chair and laced his fingers across his gym-taut belly. "So ask away. I've got things to do, so make it snappy."

"So, Malcolm, who at Quasar is trying to set Nigel up?"

Malcolm nodded in approval. "Straight to the point. I like that." He steepled his hands in front of his face, debating on how much to tell Sebastian. "If I told you that I had suspicions, and that Nigel would be cleared but that the problem was best handled in-house, would you let it go?"

Sebastian shook his head. "No. My cousin's life has been turned upside-down. He didn't deserve this."

Malcolm nodded again. "This is a very sensitive matter, Scott."

"You can call me Sebastian, since we're on a first-name basis now."

Malcolm chuckled. "Fine, then, Sebastian. As I was saying, this is a very sensitive matter. To tell you, as a representative of the DEA and relative of Nigel, my suspicions would bring additional unwanted scrutiny of Quasar."

Sebastian frowned. "Is the sensitivity due to the upcoming IPO offering?"

"That's part of it." Malcolm gave an imperceptible nod and an intense stare.

Sebastian noted the nod; what was Malcolm trying to tell him? "Or is the sensitivity due to a person at Quasar?"

Malcolm continued to stare. "Keep going."

"Let's go three for three. The sensitivity is due to a high-ranking person at Quasar."

Malcolm nodded. "Good. Keep going."

"Well, if it's a matter of sensitivity, then we're talking about someone in the upper ranks of the company. The executive team, which includes you."

"Correct."

Sebastian pursed his lips. "Is it you?"

Malcolm raised his eyebrows. "Would I be sitting here, answering your questions, if I had something to hide?"

"Yes."

Malcolm laughed out loud. "You must keep suspects on their toes, Sebastian. And you are absolutely correct." Malcolm's grin died. "But I didn't have anything to do with Nigel's setup. I have nothing to gain from him not being here."

"So you do admit to it being a setup?"

Malcolm let out an exasperated sigh. "Come on, Sebastian. You wouldn't be here if you hadn't thought it yourself. Nigel is not stupid, but he's also not the brightest bulb in the lamp. He's an underachiever, as you've probably figured out by his résumé. He really has no place in investment banking, and not in the position he currently holds; but we needed the connection to Pierre International." Malcolm picked up his Montblanc pen and twirled it between his fingers. "Drug trafficking requires long-term planning, strict organization, and a killer instinct. Those are traits that Nigel does not possess. And he makes a decent salary, but nothing spectacular. So how could he afford the payoff on eight keys of some sort of cocaine blend?"

"He could have savings," Sebastian argued.

"Please." Malcolm snorted. "Nigel brings his lunch almost every day. He lives in a borderline run-down area of Brooklyn. His suits are off-the-rack from a discount clothing chain. His shoes aren't much better. He has two children under the age of three, and a wife who does not work outside of the home, and who seems to have expensive tastes. You do the math."

"What do you mean, Nigel's wife has expensive tastes?" Sebastian racked his brain but could not recall Priscilla being into the high-post lifestyle, or any family rumors about it. Her clothes and hair were ordinary, as far as he could tell, as were the kids' clothes. The only extravagance seemed her engagement ring, and even that was over two years old. Maybe he needed to ask his mom about that.

"Maybe I'm not the one you should be asking."

Sebastian eyed Malcolm. "Then who should I be asking?"

Malcolm smirked. *"Cherchez l'homme."*

Sebastian racked his brain for a clue from his high school French lessons. "Who's the guy? Does he work for Quasar?"

Malcolm smiled. "Time's up."

THIRTEEN

Sebastian filled Alex in on his talk with Assata, including the part about her and Nigel having an affair. He also told of his impromptu meeting with Malcolm.

"Well, look at you," Alex grinned. "Mr. Investigator. Good job. As for Nigel and this Assata, all I can say is, damn! It looks like I have vastly underestimated him."

"I'm not going to be here much longer, so I have to hustle to find out anything to help Nigel."

"Yeah. I found someone who may be willing to take over Nigel's case, since I'm flying back to L.A. tomorrow. She's waiting for his call." He leaned back in his chair and stared at the ceiling. "In the meantime, we don't know who the guy is that Priscilla is allegedly messing around with."

"I think Malcolm knows, which makes me think that it's someone at Quasar."

"Then why not rat the guy out? Isn't that how it's done in Corporate America? I mean, everyone has an agenda. The fact that Jennings even mentioned this guy, says that he's got an axe to grind with someone at Quasar."

"Oh, I have no doubt that Malcolm has an agenda," Sebastian agreed. "But you have to understand how someone like Malcolm thinks. He's not going to want to get his hands dirty. He'd rather leave crumbs and let someone else follow them to the final destination.

Then, when the shit hits the fan, he can honestly say that he didn't do it."

"And come out smelling like a rose." Alex chuckled. "Semantics and plausible deniability. I love it." He shot Sebastian a sly look. "You seem to have a good handle on how Jennings thinks. You might be in the wrong line of business. Maybe it's time to dust off that MBA and come back into the family fold."

"Ha ha."

"I got in touch with a private investigator in New York, who was referred by the PI I usually use on my divorce cases. He did some digging and found some more interesting news. Priscilla is listed on a joint checking account at Commerce Bank with Nigel Pierre. And she has a separate account at Fleet Bank, and another one at Chase."

"Hmm. A bit strange for what I know of Priscilla and Nigel, but not uncommon."

"No, it's not. But the Fleet account shows a Priscilla Pierre listed as primary."

Sebastian made a "so what" gesture.

"Well, it seems that the account is a corporate account, for NTJ Holdings. When we pulled the paperwork, the principal is listed as one Trey Jacobson. "Alex straightened in his chair. "And there have been regular deposits from the Fleet corporate account into her personal checking account at Chase. Checks, which were traced back to the Fleet account and NTJ."

Sebastian stared at Alex. Priscilla and Trey Jacobson? He never saw that one coming, although Assata had mentioned that they'd seemed awfully cozy at a company picnic. "It makes a scary kind of sense. Priscilla would have access to Nigel's workspace, and no one would question it. But why would she be working for, or with, Jacobson?"

"Doesn't Nigel work with Jacobson at Quasar?"

"Kind of. Remember, Nigel said that he mainly worked under Malcolm at first, but does work for Trey and anyone else when Malcolm is out of town."

"So now we have to figure out why Jacobson would want Nigel out of the picture," Alex mused.

"Well, if Nigel found out that his wife was getting her swerve on with Jacobson, Jacobson might want him gone to keep his mouth shut," Sebastian offered.

"But Nigel is a lower-level exec," Alex argued. "Jacobson is a junior partner, and the boss's son. If push came to shove, who do you think would be believed?"

Sebastian thought about Priscilla and his suspicions of drug use. "I think that Nigel stumbled across something that he wasn't supposed to know." He updated Alex on his most recent conversation with Nigel, and the information that Jonathan had relayed about Nigel's résumé, plus the west coast-east coast connection from Zachary.

Alex nodded and stroked his neatly trimmed goatee throughout Sebastian's recital. . "That makes a lot of sense. Fraudulent loan deals to get up the cash to buy drugs, and expansion into New York in exchange for money laundering privileges."

"And using the firm's funds as a cover," Sebastian added. "Smart, but dumb at the same time. A random audit would have caught it, unless he had someone in Accounting to finagle the numbers and make it look right."

"Then how come Jacobson hasn't been caught yet? From all accounts, Jacobson is a brat who's trying to be a big dog in his daddy's firm, even though he really doesn't have the skills. And brats throw tantrums and make mistakes."

Sebastian thought about his last conversation with Malcolm. "Who says he hasn't been caught," Sebastian said slowly. He leaned forward earnestly. "Remember what I said earlier, about Malcolm having an agenda and leaving a trail of breadcrumbs? I'll lay coin that he knows something about Jacobson, but is very aware that Jacobson is not only the boss's only child, but also that the firm is about to undergo an IPO. Malcolm is already doing damage control behind Nigel's arrest."

"So let Nigel take the hit, knowing that if Nigel had a good lawyer, evidence could be dug up to show that Jacobson is the criminal, not Nigel," Alex joined in, "and would be the ones to break the bad news to Daddy, instead of Malcolm."

"And Malcolm comes out on top." Alex shook his head. "Wow. That's just beautiful. Slightly risky, but beautiful. Malcolm gives a whole new meaning to the term 'Machiavellian.'"

"That's one of the commandments of business," Sebastian said. "'Thou shalt not get caught.' And the other one is, 'Thou shalt cover thy ass.'"

"Truth. But what about Priscilla? What's her angle?"

Sebastian rubbed his earlobe as he debated on what to do with an item he acquired.

Alex noticed the gesture. "What did you do?"

"Huh?" Sebastian feigned innocence.

"Don't even play that with me, homie. We go back like spinal cords and car seats, to freshman year at Yale. Now tell me, what did you do?"

"I..." He huffed. "Can your investigator get something tested in a lab?"

Alex raised an eyebrow. "Maybe. Probably."

"Be right back." Sebastian jogged upstairs to his room, where he retrieved a balled-up handkerchief from his carry-on bag. He returned back to the den, where he handed it to Alex.

Alex unfolded the handkerchief to reveal a gold-toned plastic lipstick tube. "You want lipstick analyzed?"

"Look inside."

He used the edges of the handkerchief to open the tube, and stared at the contents. He looked back up at Sebastian in amazement. "Is this what I think it is?"

"I think so. I need the lab to confirm."

"Who did you get this from?"

"Priscilla."

"No shit?" His eyebrows raised. "I don't want to know how you got this," Alex said as he refolded the handkerchief over the tube. "And this is probably inadmissible. Actually, I'm sure it's inadmissible."

"But if you know, you might be able to get the DEA to look in another direction, enough to get Nigel off."

Alex shook his head. "I don't know. I'll go call my guy right now, see what he can figure out. But it might take a day or two."

Sebastian just had another idea. "Wait a minute. We may be able to get results sooner than that. Is Dante still here?"

"Yeah, he's downstairs in your dad's workshop. Why?"

"Tell you later." Sebastian took the handkerchief from Alex and went to find Dante. As Alex said, he was downstairs with Stephen Scott in the room he'd converted to a workshop. Stephen liked to build wooden boxes, bread boxes, bird and doll houses, and the like. He made a nice side hustle from people wanting to buy his goods, which supplemented his retirement pension from thirty years of service with Con Edison as a mechanical engineer. Dante looked up from watching Stephen's progress on a small dollhouse for Gracie when Sebastian appeared.

"Hey, son," Stephen greeted without taking his eyes off the wood inlay he was gluing to the side of the house.

"Hey, Dad. Dante, could I speak with you for a minute?"

Dante rose and followed Sebastian out of the room. "What's up?"

Sebastian lowered his voice. "Can you test a drug sample?"

Dante answered in equally low tones. "Probably. What is the sample supposed to be?"

"Blizzard."

Dante raised an eyebrow. "Where'd you get the sample?"

"Does it matter?"

Dante stared at Sebastian. "How soon do you need it?"

"Five minutes ago." He handed Dante the balled-up handkerchief. "Don't lose that. It's all I have."

"Dante saw the urgency in Sebastian's expression. "Alright. I know where to go to get what I need. I'll be back shortly." Dante bounded upstairs and Sebastian heard the front door open and close.

FOURTEEN

The family gathered for one last meal with everyone there. Several family members were leaving the next day, including Sebastian, Alex, Jonathan, and Dante. Papa and Nana Pierre would leave at the end of the week, as would Victoria, her husband Reginald, and Regina. As Rachel, Tia, and Tracey helped Janelle and her sister clear the table at the end, the doorbell rang, followed by rapid knocks on the door.

"Who could that be?" Janelle asked as Stephen went to answer the door. He returned with a phalanx of uniformed New York Police Department members, as well as two DEA agents. She gasped as the law enforcement officers filled the living room. "What is going on?"

"Ma'am, we have an arrest warrant," the tall, Hispanic agent said. He gestured to Stephen, who was reading the official document.

Nigel's throat closed up in fear. He recognized those agents; they were the ones who'd arrested him last week, at Quasar. Were they here to take him back to jail? He watched in trepidation as the shorter, Asian agent walked toward him...and placed a hand on Priscilla's upper arm, where she sat beside Nigel at the dinner table.

"Priscilla Pierre," he said in a voice reminiscent of the late Barry White, "you're under arrest for conspiracy to commit a felony, accessory to drug trafficking, possession of an illegal substance, accessory to money laundering and wire fraud." He hauled Priscilla up from her seat. "You have the right to remain silent..."

As he went to pull her arms behind her back, Priscilla made her body go limp, then twisted out of his grip and made a run for the door. Shouts of shock and disbelief formed a cacophonous background to her attempted escape. The Hispanic Special Agent intercepted her, but Priscilla was like a cornered animal. She swung and clawed at him in her desperation to escape. One her blows caught the Special Agent in in the corner of his mouth and he reared back. For a small woman, Priscilla was strong, and it took considerable effort for both Special Agents to wrestle her to the ground with her hands behind her back. The Asian Special Agent finished reciting the Miranda before he expertly frisked Priscilla and found a small pillbox in her pants pocket, which he opened to reveal iridescent white powder. He dipped the tip of a pinky finger in it, and touched that tip to his tongue. He nodded at his partner, and they lifted Priscilla to her feet before marching her out of the house. Priscilla looked back to see the horrified, angry and pitying glances of the Pierre clan. She looked at Nigel, who had tears in his eyes. She held his gaze until Nigel turned away.

Sebastian caught Alex's gaze, and Alex nodded. Sebastian nodded back. When Dante returned the previous afternoon with the positive results of Blizzard in the lipstick case, Alex made a bunch of calls and arranged a meeting with the DEA agents who were in charge of Nigel's case. Once he gave them a nudge in the right direction, and once Nigel had been broken the news of the extent of Priscilla's betrayal, they didn't have to work that hard to find compelling evidence to arrest Trey Jacobson at the same time they arrested Priscilla.

Sebastian looked over at Nigel, who sat at the table, hugging his children as if someone would try to take them from him. Silent tears tracked down his face and dampened Maya's hair. He opened his eyes and Sebastian had to turn away from the anguish there.

Family members clamored for an explanation from Nigel, Sebastian, Stephen, Alex...anyone would could possibly shed light on what just happened. It was Nigel, though, who put the children to bed before explaining about the fraudulent loan swaps, the drug trafficking through the firm by the owner's son, and Priscilla's quest for money. He also mentioned that he'd been planning to divorce Priscilla, as he'd met someone else who was more suited to him.

As the latter statement added more fuel to the conversational fire, Sebastian could only chuckle and shake his head. Family...gotta love 'em.

~~~

Later on that evening, after everyone had finally left, with bellies full of food and tongues filled with gossip for years to come, Sebastian was packing his things when Nigel knocked on his bedroom door. "Hey," Sebastian greeted.

"Hey," Nigel replied. He looked at the open suitcase. "You about packed?"

"Yeah."

Nigel nodded. He fiddled with the hem of his jacket. "Uh, Sebastian, I just wanted to say thank you. For everything that you did."

Sebastian shrugged as he rolled up a pair of slacks. "No problem."

"No, it was a problem. You were supposed to be on vacation, and instead you got sucked into my drama."

"Well, it all worked out fine. As for the vacation, well," Sebastian shrugged, "it be's that way sometimes." He folded a shirt with care. "So, how are you holding up?"

"Okay." Nigel watched Sebastian as he smoothed and folded. "The kids keep asking about their mommy." He sighed. "It's hard."

Sebastian nodded. "Are they okay otherwise?"

"Oh yeah. They're eating and sleeping well, no problems there."

Sebastian tossed his Dopp kit into the suitcase. "And Assata?"

Nigel looked at Sebastian with a startled look. "Assata?"

"Yeah. What's up with that?"

Nigel looked at the floor. "I don't know what you're talking about."

"Come on, Nigel," Sebastian said in an exasperated tone. "Give me some credit. I copped to that a while ago. Not to mention, Assata told me about it."

"Oh." After a pause, he said, "Well, we're doing okay. Taking it one day at a time, and all that."

Sebastian smiled. "Are you in a relationship or a twelve-step program?"

"Sometimes they're one and the same." The cousins exchanged laughter. "Seriously, though, she's good for me. I just hope that I'm good for her."

"She strikes me as the type of woman that would let you know if you weren't."

"True." Nigel sat in silence a bit longer, then stood to leave. "Well, I just wanted to say goodbye, and thank you again. I'm not in jail because of you, and I appreciate it. Really." He paused, then said, "Look, Sebastian, we've never really gotten along before. But now that we're older, and after all this, well..." he swallowed, "I was wondering if maybe we could try to be friends."

Sebastian stared at Nigel, then nodded. "Sure. We could try that."

"Okay." Nigel hesitated, then walked to Sebastian and gave him a hug. "Thank you," he whispered. Sebastian returned the embrace, unexpected tears pricking his eyes. The cousins released each other and Nigel walked toward the door. "See ya," he said as he gave a half-wave and left. Sebastian shook his head and finished his packing. Wonders never ceased.

Early the next morning, Sebastian walked into the living room to say goodbye to those relatives that were leaving to their respective homes, and to those who were remaining. He hugged his grandmother. "Bye, Nana," he whispered in her ear.

Nana Pierre returned his hug with a strong one of her own. "Goodbye, Sebastian. You did a good job, and I'm proud of you. And the next time you take a vacation, you need to come home to Trinidad."

"Yes, Sebastian," Papa Pierre boomed as Sebastian released his grandmother and was swallowed up in his grandfather's embrace. "You come down there, now. I got some business things I want you to check out."

Sebastian waited for his grandfather to release him so that he could breathe again. "Okay, Papa, but don't you think that Jonathan would be better suited for that?" he asked in a winded voice.

"I want you to do it." Papa Pierre was uncompromising.

Sebastian sighed; he knew that his grandfather would never stop trying to get Sebastian to formally join Pierre International. He would have to make a trip to Trinidad within the next couple of years or so. "Okay, Papa."

Sebastian grabbed Tia in a bear hug and placed a loud smack on her cheek. "Bye, Brat. Behave yourself."

"You behave yourself," Tia laughed as she returned the hug. "I'll miss you. And don't go out on any more weird dates." Sebastian had once gone on a date that had been arranged through a dating service, which resulted in him begging Tia to call him so that he could escape the date under false pretenses.

Sebastian turned to hug his father. "Bye, Dad," he said. "I'm sorry we didn't get to spend more time together."

"Things were different this time," Stephen said. "But I'll see you soon enough." At Sebastian's inquisitive look he explained, "Your mother and I are getting iPads. We can iFace."

Sebastian bit back a grin. His father could barely send an email. "FaceTime, Dad."

"Oh. Okay." Father and son exchanged similar chuckles.

"Come here to me, Sebastian," Janelle said. She wrapped her arms around his midsection and squeezed. "It was good to have you home. And thank you for helping Nigel."

"You didn't leave me much of a choice," he said wryly as he looked into his mother's grey eyes.

"No, I didn't," she admitted. "But Nigel needed the best to help him, and you are the best. And I'm not just saying that because I'm your mother."

"Mom..."

Janelle took Sebastian's face between her hands. "I am very proud of you, Sebastian Stephen Scott. " She placed a kiss on his cheek. "Now, you be safe out there."

"I will."

She turned her attention to Alex. "I'm proud of you too, Alexander." She gave him a hug and kiss as well. "Both of my sons came through when I needed them. Not that I expected any less."

Alex blushed, which was a rarity for him. He turned to give Stephen a quick hug before saying the rest of his goodbyes.

Sebastian, Alex, Jonathan and Dante gave one last wave goodbye and carried their bags to their respective rental cars, except for Jonathan, who was riding with Sebastian. All of them had flights leaving around the same time, and Jonathan surprised Sebastian with the news that he was going to San Francisco as well, on the same flight.

Dante raised an eyebrow. "I thought you were flying back to London?"

"Not right now. There's a conference for Asian investors in San Francisco, that I'm registered to attend."

"I thought you were on vacation."

"I am, but part of the three weeks I'm gone is for holiday, and part for work."

With one last honking of horns, the men left and followed each other to John F. Kennedy Airport. After dropping off their rental cars and taking a shuttle back to the main terminal, they said their goodbyes.

"I'm on Delta," Alex announced.

"JetBlue," Dante added.

"We're on American," Sebastian said.

"I upgraded your ticket to first class with some of my frequent flyer points," Jonathan told Sebastian. "Consider it a bonus for getting Nigel cleared of those ghastly charges."

219

"First class?" Sebastian grinned. "Aren't we fancy?"

"It's the only way to fly. Or, at least, business class."

The men exchanged final hugs, fraternal handshakes, and promises to keep in touch before they went their separate ways. Even Sebastian and Dante managed a hesitant hug. As Sebastian and Jonathan walked through the American Airlines terminal, Sebastian looked back through a window to the buildings of Queens. It was good to be home, but it was also good to leave.

~~~

SHOUTOUTS, THANKS, & ACKNOWLEDGEMENTS

Thanks to God, without Whom nothing would be possible.

Thanks and much love to the Davis, Booker, and Ramsey families for the support. Two snaps up in a sine curve to my mom, Robin Ramsey-Dunn, and grandmother, Esther P. Booker Ramsey.

Many thanks to Special Agent Matthew Barden of the Drug Enforcement Administration, Washington, DC Field Division, for insight into the life of a DEA Special Agent in the field. Any expertise is his; any errors are mine.
Shoutout to Torraine A. Williams and Linden J. Houston, for reading this when I first wrote it back in 2005, and giving feedback on Sebastian and the Pierre clan (Linden, you can stop re-reading your copy of the draft now LOL). Nine (!) years later, shoutout to Corregan G. Brown for reading the last two drafts and bringing it over the finish line in the clutch. You guys are money from the three, in a tied game, with two seconds on the clock.

Shoutout to Victoria C. Osborne, Dani Jackson, Carol Huh, and William Demps for checking on me offline, while I was MIA trying to finish this book.

To my Twitter tribe: thanks for the Thursday night hijinks while we live-tweet *Scandal* and *How To Get away With Murder*. #TeamFranksBeard A pack of apple Now & Laters to @BlackGirlNerds, @DawnGibson, @itsdonte, @TheJoeMorton and @JoshMalina for the pure comedy.

To my National Novel Writing Month (NaNoWriMo) and National Blog Posting Month (NaBloPoMo) folks, especially the NaNoLanta group: let's keep it going. Three more weeks! Thanks to all who have followed my blog, Tweets, and YouTube channel, and have given encouragement.

To whomever feels left out: thank YOU, _____, for your love, support and encouragement. I couldn't have done it without you.

Thanks for stopping by.

About the Author

Tee Emdee is the pen name of a cult-favorite fiction author, under which she writes thriller/suspense novels. A graduate of Georgetown University, she resides in Georgia with a room full of books, a steadily increasing collection of culinary gadgets, and a polydactyl (Hemingway) grey tabby. You can find Tee Emdee hanging out at online workshops such as NaNoWriMo and Clarion, when she isn't paying homage to her past career as a chef by whipping up homemade goodies.

Visit her on the interwebs:

Blog: www.tiffscribes.com
Twitter: @tiffscribes
Facebook: facebook.com/tiffscribes
Amazon: amazon.com/author/teeemdee